The River at Green Knowe

ODYSSEY CLASSIC

The River at Green Knowe

L. M. BOSTON

Illustrated by Peter Boston

An Odyssey Classic
Harcourt Brace Jovanovich, Publishers
San Diego   New York   London

Library of Congress Cataloging-in-Publication Data

Boston, L. M. (Lucy Maria), 1892–
The river at Green Knowe/L. M. Boston; drawings by Peter Boston.
p. cm.
"An Odyssey classic."
Summary: An English girl, a Polish refugee, and a displaced boy from the Orient explore an island-strewn river near the ancient manor house, Green Knowe.
ISBN 0-15-267450-0 (pbk.)
[1. England—Fiction.] I. Boston, Peter, ill. II. Title.
PZ7.B6497Ri 1989
[Fic]—dc19 89-2071

Printed in the United States of America

A B C D E

The River at Green Knowe

Three Children Arrive at Green Knowe

"When do the children come?" asked Dr. Maud Biggin without looking up, as she licked her thumb and flicked over the pages of one of the many books open before her. The room was full of tables, collected from all over the house, and every table was piled with books, supplies, photographs, and boxes, which spread and spilled over onto the floor. Dr. Maud was a shortsighted woman who never straightened her back, but moved about at the right height for consulting other books wherever she had laid them. When not reading, her attention was on the ground as if expecting that something very interesting there might catch her eye. She had spent much of her life digging up old cities and graves in deserts and shaley hillsides, and had got into the habit of searching the ground for fragments. She could not bear a vacuum cleaner because it left her nothing to look at. Her shambling way of walking made her look rather like a monkey, and if a chimpanzee were let loose in a shop to choose its own clothes, it would choose much the same as she was wearing. When she needed more books, she brought out a little motorcycle with a large basket on the carrier and set out for the library. And very funny she looked in her crash helmet!

"Ah! The dear children!" replied her old friend, Miss Sybilla Bun. "They arrive at teatime. I have made a three-tiered strawberry cream sponge for them. I hope they have healthy appetites. I am looking forward to seeing them eat." Miss Sybilla's only remaining passion in life was food. She liked a lot of people to cook for, because that meant she could be ordering and cooking and seeing around her much more food, heaps of food. She loved to see it going into mouths. In that respect the children were likely to have a wonderful time if their digestions were good enough. Sybilla Bun, needless to say, was very plump. She was not unlike a hen in many ways, especially on the rare occasions when she ran, for instance, after the bus. She chortled over her food and sometimes bowed gravely to it several times, looking at it first with one eye and then with the other before she ate. Her clothes were all fuss and flummery, weighted down with mixed necklaces of every kind from golden sovereigns on a gypsy chain to ivory and ebony rosaries and even melon seeds dipped in silver paint.

These two ladies had rented for the summer a house called Green Knowe in the country beside a broad, slow-flowing river. Maud Biggin had chosen this remote and ancient place because she was writing a book. (She was one of a group of scientists who believed there had been prehistoric giant men as well as giant animals.) When she had settled in at Green Knowe and had taken in its Grimms' fairy tale quality and felt how much room there was to spare, she threw off one of her ideas. She often launched an airy plan into action and then returned to her books and left the plan to work itself out as best it could. "We will send to the S.P.S.H.D.C. for some children," she said.

"The what, my dear?"

"The Society for the Promotion of Summer Holidays for Displaced Children. We will have two sent, and I will invite my great-niece Ida to take them off our hands."

"What if they can't speak English? I know *you* can speak German, Spanish, Russian, Latin, Greek, Hebrew, Arabic, and the most important words in a dozen more languages, but Ida can't. And I can't ask them if they like grilled kidneys in Hebrew."

"Don't fuss. I want to get on with my writing. I'll say they must speak English."

"But my dear Maud—is it wise? What are they going to do? Because after all there's always spare time in between meals. We've no toys, no playroom. What will they play?"

"You can't stop children playing. They'll play all right. There's the river, isn't there? And a house you can hardly believe in when you see it. What more can a child want? Just turn them out—so long as they don't interfere with the Ogru." (This referred to Dr. Biggin's book, which was to be called *A Reconstruction of the Habits and Diet of the Ogru: A Summary of Recent Discoveries*.)

"But will it be safe?" Miss Bun persisted. "Supposing they can't swim?"

Maud Biggin tossed across the letter she had just typed.

"For heaven's sake! How you fuss! Put a P.S. that they must be able to swim. And now please let me get on with my work."

Miss Bun took the typewritten note and added in her fat, round writing, "P.S. It's imperative that the children shall be able to swim. The river here is *very* dangerous."

The society had replied that they would be happy to send two children.

"Ah, here's the taxi! Here they are!" cried Sybilla Bun. "And ready for their tea, I hope. Come in, children, come in."

They stood shyly in a row. Ida was eleven, trim, gray-eyed, and reliant, but so small her age was almost unbelievable. Next to her stood Oskar, also eleven, leggy and head in air with an obstinate thrust

in his lips and chin. He clicked his heels together
and introduced himself.

"Oskar Stanislawsky."

Lastly there was a slim nine-year-old with an
Asiatic face.

"What's your name, dear boy?" Miss Sybilla
bent down to bring her nose level with his, so that
her beads fell forward and the melon seeds hung
like a skipping rope between them.

The boy gave a gurgling sigh.

"Come, tell Auntie Sybilla your name, love."

He replied with exactly the same sound.

"Doesn't he speak English?" Miss Sybilla asked
Ida. "We said they were all to speak English. What
is his name?"

Ida, though so small, was clearly the head of
the group and had established her position on the
journey.

"That is his name, that he said. It is spelt H S
U, and it can't be said in English. So we shall call
him Ping. He speaks English very well, only he
hardly ever speaks."

Ping had black velvety eyes and a delicious
smile.

"I thank you for your very kind invitation," he
said softly, with a little bow over his folded hands.

Maud Biggin, coming to the door of her study, looked out.

"How d'y' do, Midget," she said. "You don't grow much."

Ida came forward and, after a moment's hesitation, because her great aunt's bent position brought her cheek within range, gave her a dutiful kiss.

"I'm not a kissy person," said Dr. Biggin, "but I'm glad to see you. Hullo, boys. I hope you won't be any trouble. Enjoy yourselves. Be off now with Miss Bun. I'm busy." She firmly closed the study door between them.

"Come, children, with Auntie Sybilla and see your room."

As they wound their way upstairs after her, the children were wide-eyed with surprise. "Is it a Buddhist monastery?" asked Ping.

"It could just as well be a Crusader's castle," said Oskar.

"I wish I had hair long enough to let down out of the windows for you two to climb up," said Ida, shaking her two little pigtails, properly so called, for they were no longer.

They were to share a large attic room at the top of the house. It had windows on three sides, out of which they could see the river as if on a map. It

7

eautiful river, flowing through meadows or
rees. On a summer evening such as this, it
smooth, sleepy, and timeless. But it was a
willful river, ready to overflow its banks after any
heavy rain even in summer, for which reason there
were neither factories nor houses along this part of
its winding course to the sea. If after several years
of low rainfall people began to forget the past and
put out plans for building housing estates on the
meadows or factories on the banks, the river would
suddenly wake up, turn over in its bed, and pour
deep lakes of water over half the country. However,
the island on which Green Knowe stood was slightly
humped, just enough to keep it clear of the floods,
and that is how there came to be such an old house
on it.

"What a lot of islands the river makes," said
Ida. "We are on one, and I can see at least three
others. We must go exploring and sail round them
all. Perhaps we shall find one where nobody has
ever set foot. It looks beautifully wild." The boys
leaned out at her elbows. A hundred yards upstream
there was a water gate controlling the flow into a
branch that went off at right angles. The tumbling
of the water over the bar filled the bedroom with its
daylong, nightlong sound. The main stream, undis-
turbed by the loss of half its volume, flowed quietly

past Green Knowe, throwing out as it went, in its careless liberality, a loop of water that surrounded the garden and lay close under one wall of the house.

"Look at this house reflected in the water," said Ping, calling the others to look out of the side window. "Isn't it still! I can see us all looking out of the window, but our faces wiggle as if we were eating toffee." They ran from window to window, eager to see all there was.

"The sky is so blue, I wonder why it doesn't reflect the river just as the river reflects it, like barber's mirrors reflecting backward and forward forever."

"Before it could reflect, it would have to have something dark behind it like the bottom of the river. That's why."

"Well, outer space is behind the sky," said Oskar, "and that's dark, I suppose."

"Then I don't know why it doesn't reflect," said Ping. "But once is enough really. Look at the fish rising."

"Your eyes reflect," said Ida. "I can see a tiny pink sunset cloud and a tiny green pinpoint earth. No color photo was ever so *minute*."

"I see them huge, though," said Ping. "The cloud is so big that if it was a mountain, you never could possibly climb to the top, and the earth stretches all the way to where the sky begins. Miles and miles and miles with woods and rushes and waterfalls and water wheels and nightingales and bells and singing fishes."

"I shall like that," said Ida. "We'll have to go quietly by starlight to hear singing fishes. Do you *know* there are some, Ping, or are you just thinking it?"

"My father used to say," said Oskar, gazing far away at the sun, which was shooting out rays like cartwheel spokes, "that there isn't anything real except thoughts. Nothing is there at all unless somebody's thinking it. He said thoughts were more real than guns. He got shot by the Russians for saying that. But the thought wasn't shot, because I'm thinking it now. So if Ping has singing fishes, let's try and hear some. Why not?"

"I'm in a hurry to begin," said Ida. "I *want* the river. I could eat it. Let's go down to tea. Bags I this bed in the corner." She threw her suitcase on it. "Come on!"

The children were told they were to make their own beds and keep their room tidy, but as nobody ever came up to inspect, it soon became a lively and special place. Oskar had a photo of his father that he pinned up, and Ping had a Chinese picture off

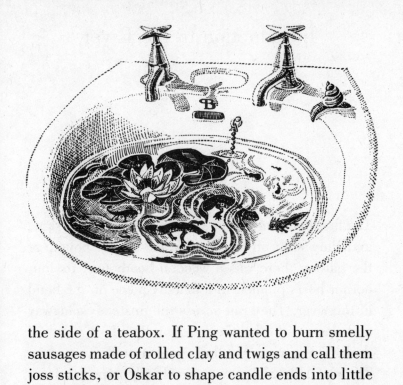

the side of a teabox. If Ping wanted to burn smelly sausages made of rolled clay and twigs and call them joss sticks, or Oskar to shape candle ends into little images of Khrushchev and stick pins into them, or Ida to keep newts and water lilies in the washbasin, it was nobody's business to know. The two old ladies fortunately seemed to think that children were as well able to take care of themselves as cats. You only needed to feed them and turn them out.

Introduction to the River

The first morning was fine and windless. Ida, Oskar, and Ping went off after breakfast. At the bottom of the garden there was a wooden boathouse, its four corner posts planted in a marshy piece on the bend of the river. They ran across the unsteady gangway and opened the boathouse door. Inside it was half dark. There was a smell of concentrated river water. The roof and walls were greened with perpetual damp and wriggly with elastic water patterns. Low down, level with their feet, a canoe lay fretting and tugging gently on its mooring. It was painted blue and brown, and the water that reflected it received it as part of itself. The canoe was lightly built and beautifully balanced, and it would comfortably hold three children. When Ida put the weight of one foot into it, it was like treading on the water itself. It yielded so far that she feared it was sinking under her, but then the water resisted, and she sat down feeling like a water lily on its leaf. The boys followed her in. Ping sat in front and Oskar in the stern. They parted the willow strands that hung like a net across the opening, and the river was theirs.

The sun had not yet pierced the haze of morning. The water was like a looking glass with a faint mist of breath drying off it. The children felt it so bewitching that without even a discussion they turned downstream, drifting silently along, willing to become part of the river if they could. Along the edge of the water ran a ribbon of miniature cliff, the top undulating like the cliffs of Dover, the vertical sides pierced with holes the size of a golf ball. Sometimes the cliff was high enough to show seams of gravel or strata of different soils. Above it willow herb and loosestrife and giant dock heavy with seed rose against the sky, and reflected themselves in the water with an effect like "skeleton" writing. The canoe seemed to hover between two skies. The banks of the river were richly alive. Moor hens hurried from side to side, trailing a widening V, fish leaped along the surface, water rats swam underwater, their V trailing from the end of their projecting noses. Or they peeped out from holes, or it might be mice, or martins, or a kingfisher. The rushes ticked like clocks; meadowsweet suddenly bowed down from above almost to the children's noses as a bumblebee landed on

it; or a rush waved desperately as something at-
tacked it out of sight at the bottom.

They drifted happily along, a twist of the paddle
now and again being enough to keep them on a

straight course. Presently the sun came out and beautifully warmed them in the shell of the canoe, and with the sun appeared another host of living things: butterflies, dragonflies, water boatmen, brightly colored beetles and lizards, and high up in the sky a weaving of swallows. The canoe drifted to a standstill.

Ping's eyes were fixed on a small spider that was descending from the branch of a tree, playing out its rope as it came, its many feet all busy. It landed on the point of the prow, made its rope fast, and immediately swarmed up again.

"We're tethered," Ping said, smiling indulgently. "Are there no big things in English rivers —no water buffaloes, no tigers in the bamboo, no crocodiles or Hippopotamuses?" As he spoke, there was a sound of a large body being jerked up out of the mud, and a shadow-flecked bullock on the edge of the bank that had escaped Ping's notice snorted in his ear. He fell over backward into Ida's lap, while the other two laughed and the bullock squared its forelegs and lowered its head. Ping stared up at it from underneath.

"I can see all of us in its eyes," he said, "reflected quite clearly. But you can see it means nothing to him. They are awfully stupid eyes. He isn't

quite sure that we aren't a dog or a motor car." Ping
stuck one leg straight up in the air. "I don't believe
he knows it isn't a stick." The bullock stared a long
time, and other bullocks came and stared too. Then
it lifted its nose and began a tremendous bellow,
which suddenly tailed off into a foolish query, mild
and puzzled. Ping put his leg down again, and the
bullock sighed deeply in relief.

"Let's shut our eyes," said Ida, "and say everything we can hear."

They all began together, so that their voices
sounded like a cluster of ducks or any other young
things that might be sunning themselves on the river.
Ida, however, said they must take it in turns so that
they wouldn't count anything twice.

Water under the canoe's ribs, whirlpool round
my paddle, drip off the end of Ping's paddle, bird
flying off tree, larks singing, rooks circling, swallows
diving, rustling in grass, grasshoppers, honeybees,
flies, frogs, bubbles rising, a weir somewhere, tails
swishing, cow patting, airplanes, a fishing rod playing out; zizz, buzz, trill, crick, whiz, plop, flutter,
splash; and all the time everywhere whisper, whisper, whisper, lap, chuckle, and sigh. If someone
moved in the canoe, a moment later on the far side
of the river all the rushes nudged each other and
whispered about the ripple that had arrived.

"Everything's trying to say something," said Ping. "Fishes poke up round mouths as if they were stammering."

"Do you think," said Ida out of a silence, "that the sound I can hear now might be singing fish?"

They all listened. There was a new sound coming from further downstream, round the next bend, a musical bubbling, warbling whistle.

With one accord all three paddles went in, and the canoe shot off. They were very vigorous after so much drifting and listening. The whistling grew louder every minute, and then appeared a huge white swan, sailing menacingly, a warship at action stations. Behind him came seven small gray cygnets, whose infant chatter was the noise that had brought the children, and behind them the mother swan guarding the rear. She now hurried forward, tossing on the water with the violence of her foot strokes, and both parents bore down on the canoe, clapping their terrible wooden-sounding wings, shooting out necks like snakes and hissing in the children's faces. Their open beaks were rough-edged mincers. Fortunately, the canoe had enough momentum to be swerved at speed to a safer distance. The mother swan turned back to her brood, and the cob contented himself with patrolling up and down between them and the fleeing canoe, keeping his implacable eye sideways to the intruders. As soon as the children felt safe, they paused to watch.

"Look, there is one tiny cygnet quite left out. It's only half the size of the others."

While the "alert" had been on, there had indeed been seven cygnets in a cluster, the smallest having succeeded in joining them while the parents' attention was elsewhere. Now, however, the mother swan had headed it off, and it swam with great agitation alone, uttering heartrending peeps. Its only and persistent wish was to join the others, but this was not allowed. Whenever it thought it had achieved its aim by sneaking round behind, a long white snake would descend, and a beak used like a spoon would flip it away.

"Why is she so horrid to it? The littlest ought to be her favorite," said Ida in distress. "She won't let it eat anything." But when the cob saw the poor little thing trying to get round behind him, he hissed and, closing his wicked mincers on its back, held it underwater.

This was too much for Ida, who leaped to her feet, nearly upsetting the canoe, and hurled her paddle. The attack and the noise—for the two boys shouted at Ida as the canoe rocked—brought the cob back to his duties. He wheeled to rap with his beak on the paddle that was now floating beside him. The poor dazed cygnet came to the surface and hurried away for dear life, straight into Ida's hands. As she had now no paddle, she cradled it tenderly in her lap while the boys worked to get out of range of the angry parent. They were not pursued. The six remaining cygnets cuddled up together and whistled contentedly. The mother swan upended herself and searched the river bottom for food. After a decent interval to cool his temper, the cob did so too.

"Their feet remind me of umbrellas blown inside out," said Ping.

The little cygnet continued to make the most mournful squeaking.

"Ours must be an orphan," said Oskar. "It's a Displaced Cygnet."

"We'll keep it and bring it up and have a tame swan swimming beside us wherever we go," said Ida. "I wonder if swans fight? Suppose it's a he-swan and there are fights whenever we go out. A sparrow fight is bad enough. Imagine a swan fight! Think of the noise their wings make taking off—like a paddle steamer."

"I don't think they fight like dogs," said Ping. "I think they wrestle, each holding the other's right wing in his beak. I would like to see it."

"It won't even be grown up by the end of the holiday," said Oskar. "It will still be a baby. And what are we going to do with it then? And where will it sleep?"

"I'll make it a nest in a box. In the cupboard there is an old eider down with a hole in the corner. We'll shake out a lot of feathers and make it feel at home."

But the grief of the cygnet was very hard to bear. It went on and on. The children could hardly talk because of it. It never stopped to take breath. It made the river journey one long execution party. The children got quite miserable.

"It will go on squeaking till it dies," said Ida.

At this point they came to a mill and a lock. The lockkeeper happened to be on the bridge, so they paddled straight into the narrow stone passage and the gate was closed behind them. As the water sank, it was like going down in an elevator. The walls rose and rose till it was frightening to believe that the river anywhere in its course was as deep as that. The cygnet's cries, magnified in the enclosing slimy walls, filled Oskar's ears like anguish in a prison. At last the gate was lifted, and after a final rush and babble of conflicting waters, the new level was established and the canoe could be paddled out into the mill pool. This was as big as a lake and as wild as a marsh. Near the mill it was overhung with trees, but its distant edge was fringed with tall rushes in which were openings where smaller streams flowed into the pool.

Just below the lock two more swans were sailing. They had none of the majesty and organization of the family upstream. They were restless, nervous, and appeared to be looking for something, thrusting their long necks at water level into the rushes, or turning round and round in one spot with necks stretched up into watchtowers.

When the canoe breasted the pool and carried the squealing cygnet into earshot, the two swans heard at once. They sailed along wing to wing, turning their heads sideways to the canoe while they circled round it. As they drew nearer, their bearing stiffened and grew fiercer, while the cygnet, now quite hoarse, yelled and fought in Ida's hands. The swans came so close, they could have overturned the canoe, their unwinking eyes level with the children's.

"What shall I do now?" Ida cried, shrinking away.

"Let it go," said Oskar. "I think these are its proper parents."

Ida opened her hands, and the cygnet, wildly scrambling on its elbowy little black legs and flap-

ping wings hardly stronger than a butterfly's, left the canoe for its mother's back. She fluffed up her wing feathers to hold it there, and both swans paddled off at full speed into the distant rushes.

"Whew! What a relief!" said Ida, but Oskar was following the course of the swans with happy eyes, his jaw thrust out.

"I suppose it got trapped in the lock the last time somebody went through in the other direction. Look, Ida, it's off her back now, and they are both showing it how to nibble water."

While they were watching, the canoe drifted into a grass bank, and Ping put his arm round a post that stood there.

"Here's a good place for mooring. Let's have a bathe." They all scrambled out onto the bank and soon had dived in like three frogs.

"I'm going to practice upending like the swans and see what I can find on the bottom," said Ida. "Let's see who can find the most interesting thing on the bottom." She vanished, leaving only her little feet and ankles on the surface. When she came up for breath, she saw Oskar's long shanks waving madly about and Ping's neat gilded legs cool like fish. At the first attempt nobody found anything. The bottom felt unpleasant to the hands. It was deep slime with here and there the rusty edge of a tin, or things that did not feel quite alive and yet moved.

"There must be all kinds of things," Ida persisted, looking—with her wet plastered hair and chattering teeth—very determined, like a hunting otter. "People always drop things getting in and out of boats. I expect this has been a mooring place ever since boats were invented. We might find Hereward the Wake's dagger."

Up came all their feet again; and again. The third time was lucky. Ida came panting to the surface with a bent piece of iron, and Ping with a live eel held firmly in both hands. When he had shown it to the others, he hurled it up into the sky, where it shone silver for a moment before entering the water again with no splash at all, like a needle entering silk. Ping seemed supremely satisfied, his almond eyes lifted at the corners, making the same kind of smile as his mouth.

"What's this that I've got?" said Ida. "It's like a starting handle. It was awfully heavy to swim with. It would be useful if we had a motorboat."

"It's a lock key," said Oskar. "Much more useful. Now we can go anywhere we want quite by ourselves."

"What a lucky find! Because this pool seems the center point for exploring lots of islands. I can see five or six waterways from here. We shall be always coming and going. What have you found, Oskar?"

"I don't know what it is—some kind of metal bowl. But it is such an odd shape—as if it really was for something special. It might be silver. Do you suppose this is all of it? It wouldn't stand steadily on this knob thing underneath. Perhaps it's the lid of something." He turned it the other way up.

"It's a helmet!" screeched Ida.

"A head lid," said Ping. "An Oskar lid."

Oskar put it on. It fitted him perfectly. As his hands passed over it, he discovered that the raised part on top he had thought was the pedestal was obviously the socket for his plumes.

They picked flowering rushes and tied the stalks into a firm base to fit the socket, and there was Oskar looking like King Arthur himself, at least to Ida's eyes. And because the helmet seemed to demand it of its wearer, Oskar stood up in the canoe all the way home—an art requiring much practice if the canoe was not to be overturned and leaving all the work to the other two. But it looked magnificent.

They were all very hungry when they got back to the house. Their first morning on the river in retrospect seemed like days. Miss Sybilla was delighted as she looked round the table from plate to plate, even from face to face, and saw large helpings of lovely food going down. But alas, Ping had only eaten half his first plateful when he put his knife and fork tidily down and, turning his black almond eyes first to one hostess and then the other, said, "Excuse me please. I beg your pardon for my rudeness, but I cannot eat any more. Already it hurts. Excuse me please."

"Nonsense, Ping," said Miss Sybilla. "I don't cook just to have it left." She piled second helpings on Ida's and Oskar's plates, which they received with willingness. "Come along, Ping. Don't disappoint me."

"Leave him alone, Sybilla," said Dr. Biggin, looking up from the book she read during meals. "Remember he's an Oriental. Look at his slight bones. You can't expect him to eat like a Teuton."

"Thank you," said Ping, holding his stomach with both hands.

For this reason Ping could never be a favorite with Miss Bun. No one in fact could compete with Oskar at table. The two ladies had not asked any questions about the morning's outing, nor did they throughout the holidays. Perhaps they thought children's occupations too foolish to interest grown-ups. Not a word was said about the lock key or the helmet. The latter was carefully cleaned by Oskar and hung up beside his father's picture as an offering.

In the afternoon the children set off again, this time going upstream. "We will make a map of the river,"

Ida proposed, "and put in it every island that we have been right round, and all the weirs and locks. It will be in colors, with little pictures of the important things. We will paint it on a roll of white wallpaper, because I expect we shall go a long way

up and down. Green Knowe will be in the middle."
Hardly out of sight of Green Knowe, they paddled
round a small island only a few yards across in any
direction on which the swan family had their nest.
The six cygnets were having an afternoon nap under
their mother's feathers. She sat erect and alert, but
the cob was off duty, lazily cruising around. The
first island on the children's map was therefore to
be Swan Island. They passed under a wooden rail-
way bridge that was built low over the water and
were lucky enough to get the thundery rumble of a
train going over just above their ears. It was a train
suitable to deep country, a ridiculous, unlikely toy
engine with freight cars, and the only train in the
day. Its squawky whistle and the drone of airplanes
so high up as to look like gnats were the only sounds
they heard that were not made by the river, as it
were under its breath, or the wild inhabitants of its
banks and pools. It seemed as though all the noise
was in the sky, and at earth level nothing but sighs
of contentment and midsummer dreaming. They were
not a talkative trio. Ida and Oskar were firm friends
almost at sight, and they both loved Ping. Ida's laugh
was like a bird's flutter, Oskar's more like a puppy's
woof. Ping seldom laughed out loud himself, but his
smile was often a reason why the others did. Gen-
erally they paddled silently like Indians. They made

their way all round a narrow island completely and thickly covered with brambles and nettles and thorny sloes that leaned out over the water. They christened it Tangle Island, and this was the first one about which they felt certain that no human being had set foot on it for as long as they could imagine. There simply wasn't room for a foot even at the very edge. Beyond this, the river divided into two. Both ways looked promising, so they went a little way up each, far enough to find that both arms divided again. It was a labyrinth of waters waiting to be explored, but it was time to turn home again. The only rule of any kind that was imposed on the children by their hostesses was that they must be in time for meals. To have been late would have caused Miss Bun real distress. Though Oskar had no sense of time whatever and Ida when she was set on one of her ideas could think of nothing else, Ping could not bear the idea of rudeness to a hostess. He felt so strongly about this that Ida and Oskar never challenged it. Miss Bun, however, gave him no credit for the good manners of all three. Ping was no eater.

Owl Palace Island and
Hermit Island

The next morning they strolled up the village street to buy a roll of white lining paper and some drawing pins. (Ida had brought poster paint and brushes with her for wet days.) They pinned the middle of the roll to the middle of their bedroom floor, so that, with Green Knowe as the center, they could unroll as much as they wanted both for upstream and down. They penciled in as much as they could remember of what they had explored already, just to make a start. Then they set off again. Each day they took a different arm of the stream, and always the best part was out of reach. Then, overnight, the holiday season began in earnest. The river was crowded with boating parties, some of whom had never been in a boat before. They shouted instructions in voices of hysteria; they went bungling from bank to bank, lost their tempers when the boat rocked under their staggers, and fell overboard amid jeers. Dogs stood in the bows and barked incessantly; outboard motors drummed and snorted past, bearing ladies who spoke shrilly to be heard above the noise. Bathers leaped from the banks dogwise, and the impact of their bodies on the water sent waves that rocked every boat and added to the din. It was no longer the mysterious river on which the children had been so entranced. True, it was winding, sparkling, and cool; the water lip-lapped under the ribs of the canoe, and the clouds had all the sky from horizon to horizon to move across. But the river had become ordinary, a playground for humans. Every creature whose real home it was had gone into hiding. It had no more private life than a swimming bath or funfair.

Ida as usual made a decision.

"All these people spoil everything. Our river is different. If we want to see it again, we shall have to come out at dawn. We'll get up every day when it is just getting light. Then we can do our exploring before breakfast and spend the daytime sleeping in the sun. We'll tell Aunt Sybilla we are going out before breakfast—we needn't tell her how early— and ask her for a thermos and some biscuits. She'll be awfully pleased when she sees how much breakfast we eat when the time comes. And if we get up really early, we'll have time to go twice as far."

Very early next morning, creeping down through a curtained house, they came out into a world that Ida hardly recognized. It felt tilted, with the moon in the unexpected side of the sky, because it was setting, and the growing light of dawn was further east than she had ever seen it before, as if the points of the compass had been displaced. The bullocks were asleep, so were the swans. No smoke came from any cottage chimney, no birds moved. A vivid red fox cantered across the field with a moor hen in his mouth. Only the water was loud. The fall at the water gates shouted carelessly to the dawn as if certain no one was listening.

The children loosed the canoe and set off, paddling expertly and swiftly because they were half afraid of such an empty world. They operated the lock for the first time, rather anxiously, with their own lock key. Both boys were eager to turn it, while Ida sat in the canoe and hoped they would not do it too suddenly so that she would be sucked down and under. She need not have feared, for it took both of them to turn it at all. They puffed and panted and stopped several times to rest. When they were all in the canoe again, they launched out across the mill pool and were caught up and whirled along in the mill race. The current pounded on the bottom of the canoe like hammers, so that it bucked and tossed. The children sat helpless and apprehensive under the unfamiliar setting moon but were carried safely into the lower reaches.

It was a dawn without sun or wind. The sky was not crowded with cloud shapes; it was just pale, the water like tarnished quicksilver and the leafy distances like something forgotten. The canoe moved in a close circle of silence, so that everything that was near enough to come within the magic circle was singled out for the imagination to play with. Such were the twisted pollard willows striking attitudes along the bank, many of them old and bent like old men, or more correctly like old men's coats, for they gaped open and were quite hollow inside, looking, as Ping remarked, ready for demons, who could step in and wear the tree like a coat at night. Ping was a great believer in demons, but the thought of them did not seem to disturb him. They were just what he would expect.

The river grew steadily wider, flowing handsomely over a clean, weedless bottom. Large trees crowded down a low hill to the edge of the water, their branches hung with hop and wild clematis. Here and there an overloaded trunk leaned out over the water at such an angle that it seemed impossible the roots could take the strain any longer. At the top of one such tree a bright yellow cat lay along the trunk, not too high above the canoe to have leaped on someone's shoulder as they passed underneath. It looked down on them with the defiant glare of a hostile cat, and the tip of its tail twitched.

"It might have been a tiger," said Ping, with that gleam of pleasure in his almond eyes that thoughts of danger seemed to bring.

The light broadened, the orange east turned to unbearable dazzle, and the water flicked off little reflections of fire. The children's eyes were screwed up against the fearful inquisitiveness of the rising sun at eye level. Ahead of them on the river's edge stood a derelict building. The walls rose up out of the water, their stones green and yellow with slime. In its welcome shadow the water too was green and yellow, but each paddle as it dipped was surrounded by a sky-colored ring. The place had so long been abandoned that it was impossible to tell for what purpose it had been built, whether house, barn, or warehouse. It had the remains of a balcony from which iron steps led down to the water, but the ivy, which once perhaps was planted to take off the newness, had for generations been allowed to grow as it pleased. Nobody cared anymore if the walls were wrapped around in a vast embrace, the windows covered, the gutters blocked, the slates lifted by prying ivy fingers. So unhampered and vigorous was the ivy that having covered the house, its stringy growth, waving in the wind and feeling for support like caterpillars at the top of a stalk, had caught on neighboring trees and wrapped them round too in its cocoon, as if the building had towers. Two windows still showed above the balcony. The sashes fell sideways, some panes were missing, and the rest were heavily curtained with layer upon layer of gray cobweb. As a last humiliation for the house, there was an ash sapling growing out of the chimney.

The children took hold of the iron rails of the steps and tied up the canoe.

"This must be where Ping's demons hide in the daytime," said Ida.

"Displaced demons," said Oskar dreamily.

"Let us visit them," said Ping.

One by one they climbed out, their rubber shoes silent on the iron, and mounted to the balcony. Having got there, they found it impossible not to turn and lean out over the river to admire the view. The wide pastures had the serenity of land that is never tended except by the refreshing floods. This expanse was the true riverbed, once a marsh extending all the way to the sea. The far side was wooded along the skyline. It was easy to imagine forest coming to the edge of the marsh.

"I don't wonder they built a house here," Ida

said. "But whatever possessed them to leave it? It seems mean, to the house."

There were double doors onto the balcony, now barred with ivy stems as thick as men's arms and much hairier. Ping and Oskar were peering between them and fumbling for a doorknob. Oskar found it, but when he turned it and pushed, the whole lockbox came away from the rotten socket and his wrist went through with it. The three children pushed on the door where they could reach it. It hung askew on its hinges and the bottom edge stuck on the floor, so that they were only able to force it open a little way.

"Ping and I can get in," said Ida, inserting herself between the ivy arms and wiggling through the door. "Oskar's too big. Ooh, it's a tight squeeze. Perhaps we can open a window for you, Oskar, when we are inside."

But it was wonderful what Oskar could do. The only part of him that gave trouble was his head, which was too wide from ear to ear. And the head can't be drawn in like the stomach.

"Of course I can do it," he said sharply to Ida, who was still talking about windows. And do it he did, his profile streamlined along his shoulder as in Egyptian pictures, while Ping watched the impossible with approving eyes.

They found themselves in what had once been a fine room. There were high windows on three sides, letting in a bottle-green light through the ivy blinds. The handsome plaster ceiling was still further decorated by small patches of twinkling watered silk where the river managed to play its flashing mirrors through gaps in the leaves. Opposite the balcony had been another pair of double doors, now missing, as were the fireplaces and all the doors in the house, so that on going through to the wide stairwell and its banistered landings, one had the impression of a continuous but much alcoved room from ground floor to roof. Cobwebs hung everywhere as if the owners had left muslin curtains to molder away through the years. Dead leaves and straw littered the floors; shiny snail tracks climbed the walls. The children crept round apprehensively, greatly oppressed by that feeling in empty houses that if you think nobody lives there, *you are wrong*. Dust and silence, and boards that creaked, not when you trod on them, but minutes afterward behind you. Ida's heart began to feel tight. She was looking across the stairs into an open doorway, where a shadow was moving on the wall, when she felt a sharp rap on the back of her hand, as if someone had thrown a pebble. Something thudded on the floor. Ida clutched Oskar, and they bent down to look.

"It's an owl pellet," said Oskar, laughing. "There must be an owl here and he spat at us."

High above them on a cornice that surrounded the base of a lantern window a kingly white owl sat, making himself in his indignation as tall and thin as a specter. When he saw them looking up at him, in a swooping and tyrannical gesture he dropped his head beyond his feet, and in that position glared at them, afterwards turning his face upside down on his neck to glare at them the other way up.

Not having frightened them away by that trick, he resumed his normal position, swaying his head from side to side and rocking on his feet.

"I believe it's his house, his very own, all of it, and he didn't invite us," said Ping. "I feel rude."

The owl, in a movement more soundless and flowing than wind or water, opened its wings and was upon them, zooming at the last moment of its dive with savage claws turned up and spread like fingers. It seemed nearly as big as Ida, its eyes far bigger than hers. It swept at them again and again, its approach absolutely unhearable and its curving flight unpredictable. They ran for the door. Ping and Ida went through like cats. Oskar had to do his conjuring trick again, Egyptian-wise, so that when his body was halfway through and helpless, his eyes and nose were still inside, turned to the owl. In this vulnerable position he saw it fly a triumphant, slow patrol over its premises and return to rest.

The children crossed over to the opposite bank and sat there considering the Owl's Palace as Ida called it.

"The ivy should be full of thousands of sparrows,

but I expect the owl has eaten them all. And all the mice too."

"Oskar," said Ping. "Can you make your face long and thin by *thinking* it?" Ida and Ping stared at Oskar in hopeful and cooperative silence while he tried.

"Did it?" he asked after a while.

"No," said Ida truthfully. Oskar felt ashamed.

Ida in sympathy changed the conversation.

"Let's see if the house is on an island. If it is, we can put Owl Palace Island on our map."

"If it's an island, it must have a bridge."

They paddled on. Sure enough there was a shallow stream, silted up and overgrown, that led round the back. There was a bridge too, rickety and rotten, barred with a tangle of barbed wire. As they went along, the channel, though fairly wide, became more and more clogged with weeds till the canoe could hardly move forward. The paddles dug into floating greenstuff that had to be pushed along like yards of sodden flannel. Obviously no boats came this way for picnics, though the big trees and the slope of the hill behind them made it a sheltered and enticing spot. With determination the children toiled at the paddles until the thought of fighting their way back again was unbearable—there was no alternative but to go on. At last the way was blocked by a submerged tree trunk, leafless, black, and slimy. It was this that broke the flow of the water and concentrated the weeds into a stagnant mass. On its far side the water was nearly clear. The children scrambled onto the bank, and using the trunk as a roller—the thick slime was nearly as good as grease—they shoved and tugged the canoe over it. In the process Ida slipped in on the weedy side and came out as green as a mermaid, and Oskar from the other side came out wearing tights of black mud. Ping remained clean and golden. It was warm enough and nobody minded being wet. The obstacle had been surmounted, and now they paddled swiftly and quietly through a tunnel of overarching elms, delighted to be back in real lip-lapping water.

Suddenly Ping, sitting as usual in the prow, made a startled sign to the others as he caught hold of a branch to bring the canoe to a standstill. Ahead of them sitting on the bank, his bare feet dangling in the water, was a strange figure. He had a brown mane over his shoulders, and all that could be seen of his face uncovered by beard or hair was the fine bridge of his nose with curving nostrils and bright eyes in skull-like sockets. He was naked except for a piece of sacking round his hips, and was as lean as a greyhound.

"It's a man-lion," said Ida.

The man was intent on his line and float and had not noticed the canoe beneath the trees. What had startled the children most was his expression, unlike any they had seen before. It was the expression of a man alone in the universe, though they could not know that.

"It's a he-witch," said Ping softly.

The man pulled in his line and sang under his breath.

"Tum túm tee úmptity úmpty eye
Tum túm titi úmptity éye."

"That's not witch music," said Oskar. "He's a displaced person that's escaped."

"Shall we go and say good morning to him? It would be polite."

They climbed out of the canoe and walked along the bank.

"Good morning," said Ping, bowing. "May we visit you on your island?"

The man looked round slowly as if he didn't believe he had heard anything, but all the same, perhaps? He cleared his throat and looked away again as if he had seen nothing, then looked back and cleared his throat a second time.

"Who may you be?" he asked a little croakily.

"We are displaced persons too," said Oskar.
"We thought you wouldn't mind."

"Have a toffee," said Ida politely, holding out
a paper bag.

"Toffee?" the man repeated dreamily. "I had
forgotten there was such a word. Toffee!" He put
out his hand to take one, but stopped to look furtively

all round as if a multitude might be closing in on him. He put the toffee in his mouth and shut his eyes while he savored it. Then opening them and jerking his teeth free from the stick-jaw, he said, "It takes me back, that does." After a while he added, "Steak and kidney pie! Bacon and eggs for breakfast! Was there really—bacon. That's a thought."

Oskar understood at once, but Ida was at a loss.

"Have you run out of bacon?" she asked.

"Have I run out of bacon?" The man began to laugh, but his laughter was out of running order. It began and stopped, it blew up and skidded into choking ha-ha's! He wiped his eyes with the back of his hand.

"Where have you nippers come from—if you're real? One's a Chinese," he added doubtfully, talking to himself.

"That's me." Ping bowed and smiled.

The man frowned.

"I've not seen a living soul for so long, I don't know what to think. But a Chinese is not likely."

"It's all right," said Oskar. "It's us, and we won't tell anybody at all. Do you live here?"

"I've lived here alone for more years than I can count. I haven't kept count. What's the use? Who wants to know? I don't. Maybe I'm an old man, maybe not yet. Would you say, now, that I'm an old man?"

"Your face is rather skinny," said Ida, anxious to give him the truth, "but your hair is quite brown and there's heaps of it. So you can't be *old* old, can you? I think you're not having enough to eat. Couldn't you get some bacon in the shop?"

"Shop!" he repeated contemptuously. "Is that racket still going on? Shops want money."

"Haven't you got any money?"

"I haven't, and I don't want any. I came here because I was sick of hearing about it. Everybody working all their lives just to get it, and everybody all the time, day in and day out, saying they hadn't enough of it. And the shopkeepers telling you what they had to pay for what you've got to pay them for. I got sick of it, I tell you. It seems funny to be talking to someone about it. I never have done all this time. Sometimes I don't know whether something I remember wasn't a dream. I used to be a London bus driver. I got so that I couldn't bear all those people, all along every pavement waiting for me in pushing crowds, always running in front of my wheels and closing in behind me, skidding in ahead of me in cars and puffing out stink. And the whole way along every road posters of people larger than life killing each other or kissing each other. I got so that I couldn't stand it. Then one day I found myself here, because it was a Bank Holiday, and this was the only place I could find where there wasn't somebody already. I had to wade through bog up to my knees to get here. And nobody's been here from that day to this, and I haven't missed them."

"I hope you don't mind us," said Ping. Ida was inquisitive, so she was less polite.

"It wasn't so very difficult to get to. What's on the other side?"

"The bog I told you of, running to the edge of a wood. There's courting couples in the wood most nights, but a marsh is no use to them. Well, I got here. And I sat down and took off my coat and shirt and lay in the sun. And the sun up in all that blue sky was my own—just for me—and the sound of the water and the leaves, rustling and stopping and rustling again. I can hear it now as if it was yesterday. I just stayed. I didn't know it was going to be for always; only when I thought of going back, I never could stand the idea. I had a bit of money in my pocket, and I went and bought an ax and some nails to build a tree house, just to pretend."

"Do you live in a tree house?" All the children spoke together, turning every way to look for it. The man looked sly.

"You see, if I had built it on the ground, some

nosey parker someday might have come asking for the rent. I wasn't to know nobody would ever come but a parcel of fairy-tale kids. It's better too for the floods. I can sit up there, above miles of flood water, watching the hayricks and planks sail by. That's a wealth of solitude."

"What did you eat in the flood?" asked Oskar, thinking of Miss Bun.

"I fished from my front door instead of from the bank."

"How do you cook in a tree house? I'd be afraid of it catching fire."

"I don't cook. I eat it raw. You needn't shudder, young lady. Have you never seen a sea lion in the zoo eating raw fish and clapping his flippers because it's so good? I just cut it into strips and let them slide down, same as he does. You see, right at the start I decided I couldn't have a fire, because smoke can be seen from everywhere. I'd have had to keep it going always because of having no matches. Sooner or later somebody would have noticed there was always smoke in the same place and have come looking for trouble."

Ida and Oskar were aghast. No fire ever, no hot soup, no cocoa, no warmth in winter, no dry clothes! But Ping said, "Lots and lots of lovely things don't want fires. Birds and donkeys and horses and cows, and badgers and hares and hedgehogs and mice and moles."

"Exactly. Just what I thought. I watched the others, and anything that they could eat so could I. In spring and summer we all live like lords. I never could fancy insects, though some find them delicious. And a man's teeth aren't really made for eating grass, not with any pleasure. Listening to sheep and horses cropping it, it sounds good, but it's a poor mouthful. But almost any new twig with a bud on it makes good chewing. Most trees have buds all winter. Elm—when you crunch you feel you're getting something. Wild rose is like apples. Every schoolboy knows young hawthorn leaves. There's wild carrot and wild spinach, and oats and clover and watercress and eggs and mushrooms and beechnuts and hazel and elderberry and blackberry. But I don't mind telling you the first winter was real hard. When everything's frozen, it's no use looking. Unless you've made a store, there isn't anything at all. And I hadn't made a store. So I did, because I had to, what bears and hedgehogs and bees do by sense. I decided to sleep it out. If they can, I thought, why can't I?"

Oskar's eyes were brilliant and big with interest. "And did you?"

"Well, young longlegs, it's difficult to say. I

4 8

haven't no calendars here, nor anybody to wake me up and say 'Hi you, it's tomorrow week.' I curled up in my house and went to sleep. And when I woke up, the frost had gone. I can't tell you more than that. But when I woke up and crawled to my door, I saw what you might call visions. They say starving people see visions. I saw things that shouldn't by rights have been there. Stags and wild boar. Often see queer things when I hibernate."

"May we please, if it isn't intruding, see your house?"

"With pleasure. *With pleasure*, ha! ha! That's what they used to say, isn't it?" He led the way, and Ping saw it first. It was in a yew tree close against the bole, thatched with yew sprigs that drooped round the walls. The door was also the window, opening halfway up the woven walls like the entrance to a tit's nest. There was no ladder. It was reached by climbing the tree.

"Ladies first," said the owner, scratching his head and laughing as he triumphantly remembered this phrase out of his far-off, incredible childhood. Ida was only too keen and might even have pushed if manners had not been established. She hopped in like a tit.

"Isn't it lovely! How clean you keep it."

"No need to live like a pig."

The house was not meant for four people. Before the others could even get in, Ida had to sit on the bed. This was a neat platform of rushes tied in flat bundles, on which lay two big sacks loosely stuffed like eiderdowns. The pillow was a smaller sack. The three children got into the bed together to try it.

"You see, I've made myself quite comfortable. It took quite a time to collect enough wool off the hedges to fill those. There was a field of sheep on the other side of the wood. I used to cross the bog by a way of my own to get there. Bulrush fluff helped, mixed in with it. And then I had a piece of luck. Two swans took to living on this bit. In the molting season they sit preening their feathers and leave bagsful on the ground. I've been very lucky. I only brought with me my knife and my fishing line, and look what I've got now." He looked round with pride. On the floor stood a tin mug, a gaily painted tin jug, a turnip chopper, a dipper full of moor hens' eggs, a bucket full of grass seeds (as if for a horse, thought Ida), a sack full of beechnuts. In one corner hung dangling a very old pair of trousers, a just recognizable busman's leather jacket, and what looked like Robinson Crusoe's coat. Oskar fingered it admiringly.

"Have you got a gun?"

"No, of course I haven't got a gun. And I wouldn't have shot the owner of that coat. That was a real nice little dog, that was. Must have got lost in the bog while his owner was courting. Got proper stuck in it and nearly drowned. So I brought him home with me, and he had a nice supper of fish, and while I was scratching him behind his ears because he was company, I noticed his coat was just ready for stripping. Just ripe and pulling out nicely. So I filled myself a bagful and turned him out lovely—long mustachios, gaiters, and riding breeches, all ready for a show. Next morning I took him across the bog, and off he went home to surprise them. Because, you see, I had had an idea. I made myself a hook out of a spindle tree, the sort of thing my sister used for making rugs for her silly little never-never house. And I took my undershirt and I pulled tufts of fox terrier hair through the holes in knots. And there you are! Keep warm in any weather and wash as easy as the dog itself. The chopper I found in a dry ditch. That was luck too—couldn't have cut reeds without it. Everything that you see came out of the river. It's wonderful what a little flood will bring down—wood with nails in it, sacks with bits of string—always useful, those two. You may have been wondering, little miss, how I sew. So did I, till I thought of persuading a horse to let me have some of his tail hairs. I don't take anything without asking. I'm beholden to nobody. The great thing is not to be noticed. What isn't noticed isn't there."

"You mean," said Oskar, "nobody's *thinking* you. Except us. And we won't tell, ever. We are displaced persons too."

"Tell us about your visions that you saw when you were starving," said Ping.

"It all looked much bigger. I could hardly see across the river, and the rushes were twice as high. It was alive with ducks. Their quacking was like a headache, so that it all seemed unreal. There were big animals wallowing somewhere in the mud, and the forest seemed to rustle and almost to talk. Then I saw a canoe nosed into the bank, empty. And I thought, 'They've got me.' But they weren't after me. They were wild long-haired men . . ." He paused, forgetting his audience.

"Like you are now," prompted Ida.

"Eh? What?" The lion-man stared unbelievingly at her. Then he put up a hand and felt his hair and looked at his thin brown legs, as if for the first time, and began to laugh.

"So that's how it is! Do you know, I still thought I was a busman! There's my coat hanging up. . . . But they had the advantage over me. *They* hadn't escaped. Nobody was coming after them with cards and papers to fill up. They were free. And they lit a fire under my tree, and a smell of roast pork came up, so that I cried like a baby. The place was teeming with animals; they could take as many as they liked. Even if I could, I wouldn't kill the few poor wild things that are left, peeping out here and there when it's quiet, the hedgehog and moor hens and herons that treat me as one of themselves. We're all that's left. Precious few fish left either. Somedays I only catch one. Better go and look at my line."

They all scrambled down, the man in a couple of agile swings. Sure enough the line was taut and pulsating. There was a biggish fish on it.

"There's my dinner for today. I'll come along with you and give you a hand over the wire upstream. You'll have left your paddle marks in those weeds where you came up. I bet you have." His voice was suddenly furious. Feeling themselves dismissed in disgrace, the children got into their canoe and paddled upstream while the man moved like a shadow in and out of the trees along the bank. They came at last to a fence of wire mesh across the mouth of the stream where it joined the larger waterway.

"Don't know what that was put there for, but it's useful to me," the man commented in a less hostile voice. "No end of things coming downstream catch on there. Push that bit of wood along to me with your paddles, will you. See, it's got nails in it. Good ones. Got to keep my eyes open. We must carry the canoe over the bank. Careful—don't want no marks. There you are. Make off now. And don't come back."

The children looked so crestfallen that the lion-man considered them for a moment with the ghost of his busman's humanity.

"I've never met three nicer behaved kids," he said. "But where one boat's been, others will follow. Let be. I've dreamed you and you've dreamed me, see?"

In the canoe Ida waved, Ping bowed, and Oskar stood up long-legged as any savage. The man stared after them for a while, then bent down over his plank, which was enriched with a good piece of wire twisted round one of its nails.

"I was thinking," said Ida after they had paddled unhappily in silence for some time, "we would go back and take him some lovely food. But I filled one of his tins with toffee when he wasn't looking."

"I put a Mars under his pillow," said Ping.

"I put an envelope of fishing gut in the pocket of his busman's coat," said Oskar. After that they all felt better.

For breakfast that day Miss Bun had cooked the most wonderful, the most mouth-watering bacon and scrambled eggs and mushrooms and fried bread. Ida opened her mouth to say something, but Oskar, thought-reading, kicked her under the table, and Ping drew a finger across his throat.

"What were you going to say, Ida love?"

"Only that I'm hungry," Ida said sadly.

Flying Horse Island

It was turning into a hot day. In the little village street there was still no one about, and smells of bacon came from the cottages. But Ida, Oskar, and Ping had had a day full already and could hardly keep awake. They had only enough energy left to find the quietest sunny bank and go to sleep there, curled up like mice. Sometimes Ida spoke into her arm, to say something like "Are you asleep?" And Ping or Oskar would answer "Yes."

They spent the hot afternoon bathing in a deep pool above the water gates. They plopped in like frogs; they bobbed like corks. Ping's face swimming looked as smooth as a sea lion pup, his velvety eyes blinking in the glitter off the ripples. Oskar's hair was always in his eyes. He reminded Ida of a wet sheep. She laughed till she forgot to treadle, and the water came into the corners of her mouth and

her grinning teeth. They came out to rest, to let their bodies steam and toast in the sun and ripen for the luxury of the cool swill of river water receiving their limbs again.

Other holidaymakers thronged the river in sun and shadow. Punts passed slowly and traveled far upstream with the tall figure poling at the stern dwindling to a matchstick. Girls lolled and dozed, trailing their fingers in the water ribboned with weeds, while young men feathered them along. Cabin cruisers chuffed majestically from distance to distance, and casual eyes looked down on three sprightly children, never guessing that for them this busy summit of the day was the hour that didn't count. Ida was saying to Ping and Oskar, "I've slept so much today I don't feel like going to bed tonight. Let's be out all night. Quite different sorts of things must happen in the dark. If we want to come out when all these people aren't there, so must other things. River things."

"Giant water snakes," said Ping. "Far more majestic than cabin cruisers. They would ride like swans pulling a whole train of their own curves behind them with all the fishes dancing ahead of them in terror. And perhaps two king water snakes will meet and have a battle. Or we could ride on their necks like elephant tamers."

"Let's spend the night on the big island opposite the house," Ida suggested. "It has notice boards everywhere saying 'Landing Forbidden'; I can't think why. And for some reason nobody ever does land. Aren't people obedient! But I'm sure whatever comes out at night takes no notice of boards. We won't. I think it ought to be a good place because *it*, whatever it is, will be used to having it to itself."

During tea the children were quiet, saving up their energy and excitement for the night. Dr. Biggin was deep in thought, studying her tea leaves or pushing the crumbs round on her plate as if she expected to find bits of the Ogru there. Miss Sybilla Bun was cooing to her food, turning the cake dishes round to look at them from all sides, bowing to congratulate the cakes for having risen perfectly. When she was icing them in the kitchen, patting and putting the last touches, the silver sweets or the borders of upended almonds, you would have thought she was dressing a child for a party, she talked so lovingly to them. When she came to cut them, it was the same again. Her knife hesitated in the air, and always as she was going to cut, she widened the slice a little and laughed merrily. So now, if biscuits and rock buns slipped into pockets in provision for the night hours, it was not noticed except that Miss Bun would say with pleased surprise, "Oh! the plates *are* emptying fast! Are you ready for the praline and coffee sponge?"

After tea the children began their map. Ida said they were not to paint any part till they were sure it was right. Then they would put in pictures to show what each island was famous for. They had marked Green Knowe in the middle and continued to extend the river on each side as far as they had gone, marking the boathouses, the weirs, water gates and locks. They were able to name Swan Nest Island, Tangle Island, Owl Palace Island, Hermit Island, and mark out others that they knew but had not been on. One of these was the large island opposite Green Knowe, where they were going to spend the night, which as yet had no name.

At midnight, when Ida woke the two boys, a dusty curtained blackness filled the house, and the cold windowpanes were all that separated them from the void outside. They put on their warmest clothes and crept silently downstairs. Although nobody had told them they were not to go out at midnight, they knew enough of grown-ups to expect to be sent back to bed if they were caught. Creaking floors and old obstinate doors and steep uncarpeted stairs had to be passed, the flashlight traveling from banister to banister till they were down on the brick floor of the hall, where all the scents of the day before were settling as mud settles in still water.

Outside it was less dark, though there was no moon or any star showing. After a moment or two the earth could just be distinguished from the unbroken cloud of the sky. It was recognizable as a huge dim mass. As the children moved uncertainly along—for Ida would not allow the flashlight because it was cheating—they could not even see the avenue of shaped bushes along the path, thought they knew when they were near one because of a looming feeling in the darkness, and a yew smell. The river, however, had a just perceptible glimmer of its own, though where it was reflected from was a mystery. In the boathouse the dark was absolute and the smell of water and rotting wood as powerful as in a forest. The familiar fidgeting of the canoe came to their ears, but they had to feel for its rim with their hands.

It seemed a long way as they paddled across the river in darkness toward a bank they could not see. The sound of the water gate was magnified to an ominous fall, much too near. It was a relief when the prow of the canoe grounded on the bank. Ida had brought her ground sheet.

"We'll sit beside the water gate," she said, "and then if we want to talk, it will drown our voices. We shan't be heard."

Their eyes were getting used to the darkness. They could see the line of foam below the fall, and the bars of the water gate showed hard and black against the soft sooty ceiling of cloud. They could not see each other except as densities. As they sat and waited, they gradually acquired a feeling of the position in space of open ground or trees, and the different kind of openness that was the course of the river.

They huddled together, overcome by the immense solitude. Or perhaps it was not solitude, thought Ida, but rather that the three of them were the only ones who ought not to be there.

"I am glad we are on this side of the water gate," she said. "If Ping's water snake comes, the gate will keep it on the other side."

"You don't know my water snake," said Ping. "It will rear up and look over the top bar and slide its body over, length after length, slippery like a waterspout, and—"

"Shut up about your water snake," said Oskar. "You'll make it come real."

"All right," said Ping. "Would you rather have a spider as big as a hay-making machine, with curved, springy legs coming up one after another, crossing the island *now*?"

"Don't!" said Ida. "That's worse. Can't you think of something nice, like your singing fishes?"

"If only it weren't so cloudy," said Oskar, "we might see two stars come from outer space and have a collision and make a blaze and falling sparks like a Roman candle. I don't know what we expect in this darkness. Even if there were a parliament of badgers, we shouldn't see it. We'd only hear the barks and squeaks. The thing is to listen. We might hear a litany of worms. Their noses would be as thin as blades of grass, and they would sway from side to side in supplication. We shouldn't see them, of course."

"What do you imagine worms would sound like?"

"Like wind through a keyhole."

" 'Thou knowest that we are but dust,' " said

Ida. "I wouldn't like to miss the worms. If we stay here, we can't hear anything but the waterfall. Let's move to the quietest place, so that if anything comes, we shall hear it."

They walked along the bank till they came to a quiet reach on the far side of the island with a gently sloping bank. There they sat down.

"What a lovely smell there is everywhere! What can it be? I have smelled it all the time since we landed here. And when I strain my eyes, there is a sort of whitish look in the air." Ida put up her hand to brush something away from her hair, then caught it and drew it down to her nose. "It's meadowsweet. This side of the island must be covered with it. How comforting! I am sure only nice things live in meadowsweet."

They sat and listened. Quiet water sighing; now and then a rustle in the reeds; in the near distance the known weirs and faster currents of the encircling water; in the far distance the screech of young owls among the trees in the churchyard.

Presently Ping said, "I can hear something coming."

They all held their breath. They heard, from a little way off, very slow footfalls, one step at a time with long pauses in between. Ping breathed, "This is it." Then they saw above the gleam of meadow-sweet a crowd of white blurs that moved dreamily up and down.

"Can it be will-o'-the-wisps?"

"With footsteps?"

For a while there was nothing but their heart-beats banging in their ears, then suddenly, close at hand, crisp, short tugs, here, there, and every-where.

"Horses!" said Ida, laughing. "Hundreds of them! The will-o'-the-wisps are the stars on their fore-heads. I never saw them here in the daytime, did you, Ping? This island's always empty."

The sky was very slowly growing less dark, as if the cloud ceiling was going up higher, leaving less shadow and more space over the featureless earth. Against this space could vaguely be seen the outline of horses' backs and necks, a big herd mov-ing along together, cropping clover and meadow-sweet as they went.

"Let's try them with our apples." The three chil-dren went out to meet the horses, but the herd with-out hurrying, without even seeming to notice them, turned aside and could not be met face to face. Running, stalking, cajoling were all in vain. The indifferent creatures kept just out of reach.

Tired, Ping and Oskar threw themselves down on the riverbank. "Perhaps they'll come down to drink," Oskar said. "What we want now is a word of power."

"Be quiet!" said Ping. "I'm listening to the river and doing magic."

Ida remained standing, her eyes straining after the horses. She caught her breath and seemed to herself to become nothing but a wire for a current of electric attention. Above the line of a horse's back *something* had flapped up and blocked out the sky for a minute. And another. And again. And there was a sound to match it.

"Ping!" she cried. "What have you done? They are winged."

And now in the glimmer of the night the horses, as if all moved by the same inclination, one after another put up their wings, pointed like yacht sails, and still browsing moved majestically on.

"Oskar! Ping! Oh, Ping!"

Ping answered, scrambling up from the position where he had been leaning over the river. "I asked the river to give me a word of power, and it answered over and over again my own name HSU." As he said it, the leading horse lifted its head in his direction and gave a docile whinny—taken up by all

the herd as they too raised their heads and drew
forward. Ida remembered the sound for months, trying to describe what it was like. The nearest she could
get was the excitement of an orchestra tuning up,
with flutes and oboes running up and down above
the buzz.

The horses, all holding their wings in the same
ceremonial position, advanced, the quickened pace
of their walking hoofs thudding on the grass. They

put out their noses with wide, flaring nostrils to Ping, who murmured his name to each in turn and received a reply very like it.

After this they accepted all the children. They let themselves be handled. They nibbled themselves under their wings. They had immensely long manes and tails, and their ears twitched like mouse whiskers. As the darkness shifted into less than dark, the children saw each other's faces and hardly recognized them. Ping stood leaning his head against the leading horse's neck, and its black mane fell round his face so that he looked like a witch girl, his teeth showing white as he smiled with great joy. Oskar looked like a lean prophet absolutely believing the impossible. He was nearly crying. Ida's gray eyes were black because they were all pupil. She was curled up between the legs of a winged foal that lay on the ground. She looked like a cat that was its stable companion. The musky smell of horse was all round them. The foal smelled young, like a puppy.

At this happy moment the wail of a distant fire siren tore the long silence of the night. Up and down, far and wide, vibrating like panic, it ripped up the space of dreams.

The horses wheeled away from the children and were off, galloping to a flying start, their wings clapping till the air was bruised. When they were air-borne, the sound had the pulse and drumming of an express train fading far away—a sound the children had often heard from their beds.

Ida wanted to say that the foal had flown with its long legs hanging down like a mosquito. But none of them dared to speak at all.

It was not until they were back in their own beds and Ida, waking up at normal breakfast time, had stretched her arms and legs and relaxed again into comfort and laziness that she dared to say, "Ping? What did you do with your apple last night?"

"The horse ate it," he replied, sitting up in bed golden and sleepy-eyed. Ida smiled. "Mine too," she said.

"Mine too," said Oskar into his pillow. So nothing more needed to be said. But when they were dressed, Ping knelt on the floor by the map, and in beautiful strokes with a paintbrush he wrote the Chinese for Flying Horse Island.

At breakfast Sybilla Bun remarked, "I don't suppose you children heard the fire alarm last night. It gave me quite a fright. I got out of bed to look."

The children's eyes all turned to fix her with a questioning gaze.

"Did you see anything?" Ping ventured.

"No. Anyway the milkman told me it was only a haystack somewhere."

Mouse Island

Dr. Biggin had received a letter from somebody called Old Harry, who, as the children already knew, was her chief partner in the excavations they had done in Abyssinia, where tools that seemed to have been made for giants had been found, and a queer bone. Old Harry wanted her to hold a meeting for their committee at Green Knowe, at which he and she would both read papers. He was also pleased to be able to tell her that, as requested, a bag containing a sample of the much discussed grass, *paradurra megalocephala Abyssiniensis Andrewsii*, would be delivered separately. "And here it is," said Dr. Biggin, picking up and shaking a parcel. "My dear," she went on, speaking to Sybilla Bun, "this is the seed that Old Harry considers the main cereal food of the giants. We think they ate it as a sort of porridge. In quantities of course. I often wonder if

Scotland might not yield some surprises if we dug there. I think if you make a little porridge every day and give it to Ida, we can measure her before and after and see if it adds anything to her stature."

"Would it not be better," Sybilla said tactlessly, "if we gave it to Oskar, as he is growing so much anyway. You would get much more interesting results."

Dr. Biggin was deeply affronted.

"You have no idea of scientific investigation at all, Sybilla. I specially chose Ida because she is *not* growing. For one thing, if she does grow, it will be as near proof as we could get. For another thing, she is much too small, so we can afford to experiment with her. It would be an improvement. Whereas the effect on Oskar might be disastrous. He might shoot into a giant before the end of the holidays."

The children were not sure if this was one of Dr. Biggin's jokes or not, but they could not help laughing. Ping put his hand above his eyes as if gazing up into the sky, expecting Oskar's face to appear there.

Miss Bun was a little hurt too. She lifted the lid off the coffeepot and inhaled the aroma with closed eyes to restore herself. Then she said, "Well, that means that dear Oskar can have some nice real porridge. I don't imagine," she added, twitching her shoulders so that her beads rattled, "that the Ogru were *good* cooks."

"The latest theory is that they lived like gods. But I admit we are a long way from having access to any of their recipes. We can guess at some. But where can you get meat on the spit now except in the most expensive restaurants? And then it is only over gas. No flavor of burned cedar in it. Gas! Pooh! But of course you have never eaten kid cooked under the stars."

"Do the stars make it taste?" asked Ping gravely.

"Eh? And why not, I should like to know! Now don't get upset, Sybilla. Nobody in England does better with our wretched modern substitutes. After all, Old Harry has suggested bringing the committee here for your cooking as much as for anything else."

Miss Bun was mollified. Smoked salmon, chicken Maryland with dry hock, crepe suzette, melon and ginger ice . . .

"It would be nice," said Maud Biggin, openly winking at the children, "if you could make us a kidney risotto with *paradurra megalocephala Abyssiniensis*. They would be interested."

Miss Bun grew crimson.

"I shall do no such thing, Maud. The most I shall do with your miserable grass seeds is a gruel for Ida. It is the domain of medicine, not of good eating. Good eating is an art."

After breakfast Ida was solemnly measured, lying on the wooden floor so that she could not cheat by stretching. After that the children were free.

They still felt that after meeting the winged horses they had had enough excitement for some time. Also, in order to cherish this secret memory and keep it from being rubbed out or discredited by the presence of humdrum holiday crowds, they decided not to go on the river at all, but simply to cross over the moat into the orchard belonging to Green Knowe and to spend the day there. Sybilla Bun had even excused them from lunch, giving them a picnic basket, because she wanted to go shopping in preparation for the committee's luncheon party.

The orchard itself was an island, connected with the garden by a rickety willow-pattern bridge. It was derelict; the trees were old and leaning. Under them the uncut grass was bulgy and soft like an eiderdown. It was bordered by a thick hedge of hazel and hawthorn and was quite hidden from the river.

The sky was cloudless, and the sun beat down with a heat that hushed both birds and humans. Oars squeaked going up the river, but the people in the boats were silent, flopping back and saving their energy. The three children lay in the grass and watched the activity taking place there. In this shady world of crisscrossed stalks the heat brought everybody out. Ants, beetles, spiders, grasshoppers, butterflies, bees, caterpillars, and the rest were all as busy in the crowded space as city dwellers. Some of the caterpillars were so stupid, it was maddening to watch them, but the spiders and bees knew exactly what they were doing and wasted no time about it. The butterflies and big sealskin-coated bumblebees were bent on pleasure only and showed that they knew it. Over all, the birds swung and peered and picked off the fattest. The grass grew high round the children's flattened bed.

"There's a little road here," said Oskar, gazing into the stalks near his face. "It looks as though it might be a mouse road. Yes, it is. There's one running along it now. It's his garden path leading to the nest. He's climbed up the stalks and gone in."

The children all watched. The harvest mouse took as little notice of them as if they had been calves or foals. The nest was woven round three strong stalks of wild barley. It was hardly as big as a tennis ball, and the mouse itself not much bigger than the sealskin-coated bumblebee. He looked all head, tail, and hands and was adorably pretty. He seemed to be collecting stores of grain to take to his mate, who now and again put her head out at the door to wait for him. Inside they could be heard talking in squeaks no louder than you could make with a pair of scissors.

"Let's see who can make the best mouse nest," said Ida, after they had watched for some time.

They all set to work. Ida had done basketwork at school, but all the same she found it difficult and fiddling and very slow. It was not beyond any of them to make the initial platform that bound the three tall stalks together, or to continue as far as an eggcup shape, but when it came to leaving a hole halfway up for the door and then closing in the roof, they were all beaten. No harvest mouse would have recognized their clumsy efforts as intended nests. Ping's was made from strong broad green grasses and looked like something a cow had dropped out of its mouth. Ida's was of straw, hard and spiky like a doll's linen basket. It was also big enough for a rook.

Oskar was frowning with concentration, his long fingers delicately manipulating fine dead grass, but in vain.

"My hands are too big," he said. "Anyway, *they* do it from inside."

"Let's have our sandwiches," said Ida. "Then

afterwards we can climb trees." She and Ping began to unpack the picnic basket, but Oskar was in one of his obstinate moods and would not stop.

"I am going to do it properly," he said. "From inside."

Ping and Ida laughed. "It will be big enough for a bear."

Oskar took no notice. He began tearing up big swathes of grass, which he wrapped round himself till he was hidden. He then turned round and round inside like a dog determined to lie down just right.

The other two were setting out the meal and joyfully drinking homemade lemonade out of bottles with straws, closing their eyes to enjoy it more. When they looked round again at Oskar, the swathes of grass were tightening up round him into a passably firm ball, from inside, which—through a hole that his hands were fashioning—they could see his face looking out.

"Doesn't he look small," said Ping. "It must be the hole working like the wrong end of a telescope."

Oskar's eyes were immensely big and bright and his nose sharp as he continued to work inside his nest, tightening it even closer round him.

"Don't you want any sandwiches, Oskar? They are lovely. And there is melon too."

"Not yet." Oskar's voice from inside sounded

faint. He grunted with effort as he turned round and round in the rustling grass ball, where every moment the space grew less.

Ping and Ida ate, putting aside Oskar's share. The melon was most delicious, and as the pips that they had emptied out dried in the sun, they were thrilled to see the harvest mouse come and take some away. Afterwards they watched the two mice at the opening of their nest holding melon pips with their hands and wiggling their whiskers as they ate.

"Oskar! Do come and look. Oskar!" There was no answer. "Hush!" said Ping. "Don't speak to him. *He's really doing it*." The grass ball had tightened up till it seemed impossible Oskar could be inside. And it was growing smaller every minute.

It was very hot. The midday siesta was on. The birds had vanished; the butterflies lay with wide-open wings, fearing no attack. The harvest mice went in to sleep. Smaller things crept under leaves. Ida and Ping were drowsy too. Looking at tiny things closely for a long time makes one sleepy. They lay back in the grass and snoozed.

Something made Ida wake with a start. A ginger cat was sitting in the grass staring with its purposeful eyes at a little ball of hay that was rocking slightly on the ground. For one second Ida's heart stood still; then she made the most tigerish sound she could and threw the vacuum flask at the cat. It fled, pursued by Ida and Ping with every stick or stone they could lay their hands on.

When they came back, Oskar was standing beside his nest. He was perfectly recognizable, two inches tall. His tiny voice came up to them. He did not seem to have noticed anything wrong.

"I've made the nest all right. It is beautiful inside. I just didn't know how to make it up on the stalks. But I see now. It's quite easy really. I'll have to begin again. I'll make one next door to the mice. Get your big feet out of the way, Ping."

"Do be careful not to tread on him," said Ida. "Isn't he *sweet*?"

"Idiot!" said Oskar. He was obviously shouting, but it was the littlest voice in the world.

They watched him make his way along, tacking and working out how to get round obstacles exactly as all the other grass dwellers do. The ants to him were as big as dogs, the grasshoppers like kangaroos. Before long he picked up a pole as big as a match to use in self-defense. When he came face to face with a stag beetle, he gave it a whack as if it were a bullock, and it veered off. He came at last, after a lot of scrambling and sprawling, to the mouse road, where the going was easier.

Ping and Ida on all fours watched spellbound.

Ping's face had his happiest golden-moon look, but Ida looked like a fox terrier whose dearly loved owner is behaving incomprehensibly.

Oskar stood at the foot of some grass stalks, swaying them to see if they were stable enough. He chose three good ones and began his second nest. To save him many laborious journeys, Ping and Ida from the immense range of their arms picked and handed him the fine dead grasses he needed. His pink hands, no bigger than mouse hands but still recognizably Oskar's, came out through the hole and took what was offered them. Sometimes he rejected them and asked for softer ones, and finally for moss. And now a second nest was swaying on its three poles next door to the mice, whose anxious faces peeped out with twitching noses. Clearly they didn't at all want a neighbor.

Oskar looked out of his door, laughing with teeth like pinheads.

"I'm hungry after all that. What is there for lunch?"

Ida felt peculiar. She broke off a corner of egg and salad sandwich and offered it on a wild rose leaf. "Oskar!" she pleaded. "*Please* don't grow wiggly whiskers! He can't drink lemonade out of the bottle, Ping—he might slip in down the neck and drown."

"I've got an acorn cup in my pocket. Fill that."

Oskar took it between his mouse hands. It was like drinking out of the salad bowl, but he was very thirsty.

"You can't think how cool and nice it is in this moss," he said. "I must just curl up and have a sleep. It was awfully hard work." His head withdrew into the nest, and Ping and Ida were left out.

"We'll have to sit and keep watch," said Ida, "because of that cat. What do you think will happen next, Ping?"

"I don't know! But I wish I had thought it too."

"Could you have done, Ping?"

"Well, I knew what he was doing. I could think it for him but not for myself."

"I can't think it at all. I'm frightened because of that hateful cat. And maybe the beetle was a blood-sucking one. Oh, Ping! There's a woolly bear going up Oskar's stalk. It's as tall as he is. Just imagine those baggy suction legs walking over you."

Ping picked off the caterpillar, and immediately it curled up into a ring in his palm.

"You see, he'd only have to give it a poke in its soft underneath and it would curl up like a hedge-hog."

"I hope hedgehogs don't eat mice."

"They eat beetles, I think. But it would be horrid if one rolled on you by accident."

They sat on, anxious and puzzled and, after a while, bored.

"I wish he'd wake up," said Ping. "I want to see him walking along the high road."

"No. He might get run over. Besides, think how slow he would be. Like going for a walk with a woolly bear."

Presently, however, Oskar put his head out and said, "I'm hungry again. What is there?"

"Apple pie, melon, and chocolate."

"I think I'll go and call on my neighbors. Break off a piece of pastry, Ida, and give it to me when I get to their door."

He shinned down his stalk and began to climb up to the harvest mice. As their stalk swayed under his weight, the mice looked out in wonder and alarm. When he was at nest level, Ida with her huge fingers handed him a fraction of pastry, which he clutched to his chest as he went in.

There was agitation and squeaking inside the nest as it swung from side to side, but after a while all was still.

"Do mice bite visitor mice, do you think, Ping? It is terribly quiet."

To Ida's great relief Oskar's face appeared.

"They are nice. They eat out of my palm like ponies. Their eyes are as big as hand mirrors, and their tickly whiskers reach across the nest. It's like being in a room full of aerials. You have to be careful not to step backwards through them. But I've combed their coats with my pocket comb, and they loved it. They lie on their backs to have their stomachs done."

In fact, Oskar was so delighted with his new view of the world that when it was teatime, he wouldn't come in with the others. "You go. Just say you don't know where I've got to. It's too nice here and too exciting. I'm going to stay. I want to explore the forest again to see woodlice like armadillos and earwigs like crocodiles. Besides, I'm going to sleep here in the moonlight."

"Yes," said Ping. "Perhaps in the night a death's-head moth might look in at your door. I do feel stupid being this size."

"Oskar," said Ida, "I won't budge unless you come with me, and that's flat. I'm bigger than you and you've got to do what I say. If you go in the grass, you could get lost, and we might tread on you while we were looking for you. Or a cat might get you and bring you in and play at killing you on the floor. Or an owl might eat you and spit your bones out in a pellet. You come with me or I'll break open your nest and catch you."

"I wish you'd go away. You talk like an ogress."

"Come with me," said Ping. "I promise to bring

you back again. You can sleep in your nest, only we must be there on guard."

"What a lot of fuss about nothing," said Oskar, stepping out onto Ping's hand.

"Besides," said Ping, looking lovingly at the little person on his palm, "think how exciting the house will look. No cathedral was ever anything like so big. The biggest cathedral imaginable would go under the table, spires and all."

Ida was miserable because Ping had got Oskar and because she had nagged just like any grown-up woman. When they reached the house, Ping put Oskar in his pocket and they went in to wash for tea. As they stood side by side at the basin, Ida could bear it no longer. "Let me have Oskar in my pocket, please, Ping."

Ping amiably fished him out. "He kicks like anything," he said, standing him on the glass shelf.

"My legs have been nearly broken by your pocket knife," said Oskar, buzzing and squeaking with annoyance. "And why do you want to fill your pocket with fossils and shells? They nearly crushed me."

"There's nothing in mine, and it's a patch pocket. You can hold onto the edge and look out. I would like to see Aunt Sybilla persuading herself she wasn't seeing you."

"I wish I was back in my nest. This is just

tiresome. I'm not going to be in anybody's pocket.
Put me down, Ping. I'm going upstairs by the mouse
route. I'll meet you there after tea. Bring me something to eat."

Ping put him down on the floor, and they watched him make his way round the side of the bath to the hole where the pipes went through the floor.

"Be sure you make plenty of noise, so that we can hear where you are," said Ida, as he lowered himself into the hole. "Promise!" she called urgently to the tiny fingers clutching the edge of the floor-board, which was the last she could see of him. The only answer was the faint scraping of his buttons as he slid down the lead pipe.

Tea was to be in the garden because of the heat. It was a blow to Ida, who would not be able to hear Oskar's progress behind the wainscot. She hated lying, but it is no use saying what nobody will believe, so she made the best of it and carelessly announced, as she sat down to tea, "Oskar said please excuse him tonight. He met a thatcher and stopped to learn how it is done. And he was very good at it, and he has stayed for tea with the thatcher."

"Oh, dear! And I have made chocolate éclairs for a treat. Who is the thatcher? Not a gypsy, I hope."

"I know him," said Dr. Biggin. "A decent sort of man. I had a talk with him the other day. It's a trade that goes back further than any other, probably that and wattle-making for the walls. Paleolithic man must have thatched where there were no caves. Very interesting survival. Surprised you two were not more interested."

"We were," said Ida. "We were terribly interested, but we were no good at it."

"Too small, I suppose. Sybilla, have you made that gruel for Ida?"

"I made a sort of girdle cake of it, Maud. It seemed more appetizing for the poor child."

"Aunt Maud!" said Ida, suddenly brightening up, "may I keep it till bedtime? I read once that we only grow in our sleep, so surely it will work better then?"

"It's never been tried before, so one experiment is as good as another. But promise me that you will eat it."

"Yes, Aunt Maud."

While they were having tea, sudden banks of cloud reared up high and toppling, one on each horizon as if threatening each other. The air had gone copper-green and electric. The wind blew first from one side and then from the other, urging the opposing storms toward each other. The leaves shuddered and showed their pale undersides; the birds hid—all except the swallows who continued cutting figures of eight at ground level till it was as dark as in an eclipse. Then the first lightning flicked like a whip and Miss Bun cried out, "Here it comes! Hurry, children, before the cake gets wet."

They ran indoors, carrying plates, and finished the meal in the dining room. Nobody talked much because of the oppression of the hush that precedes the real downpour. From time to time above the ceiling unusual slitherings and scatterings occurred, not convincingly mouselike to Ida and Ping. But Miss Sybilla cocked her head and said, "I wonder if mice come indoors away from the lightning. I never heard so many. I must set some traps."

"OH, NO!"

Miss Bun and Dr. Biggin looked at Ida in surprise.

"I love mice," she said lamely. "Besides, you might catch the wrong thing."

"Such as?"

"Such as . . . a robin."

"Or a butterfly," said Ping helpfully.

"Please don't put traps, Aunt Sybilla."

"Schoolgirl sentimentality," said Dr. Biggin with her mouth full.

It had grown quite dark. Miss Sybilla was turning on the lights, but Ida and Ping went up to the attic where they were right in the middle of the storm and could watch it out of three windows and see the lightning reflected in the river.

"Oskar's missing this," said Ida. But at that moment they heard a little fluttering noise behind the cupboard door. A clap of thunder made them jump, but when it had finished tearing and crashing, there was the impossibly small noise again, as if a fox terrier as little as a harvest mouse was waiting to be let in. They opened the door, and Oskar ridiculously walked in. He was covered with cobwebs. "Beastly stuff," he said. "It's sticky and elastic and I can't get it off. I'd hate to be a fly."

"Could you see the lightning?" asked Ping.

"Of course I could, through every crack. There were long corridors under the floors between the joists. In the flashes they looked endless and awfully ghostly. Sometimes I had to climb over beams with sides as high as a cliff. It wasn't too difficult, because fumbling about in the half-dark I could always find wormholes big enough to put my fingers and toes into. Then the lightning would come and show me myself hanging on high up, and that was frightening. Mice must be very good Alpinists. I gave up the stairs and came by the slanting water pipes, but the hot ones were terribly hot, and when they cooled down and clanked, they bucked me like a horse. What have I missed? I heard you shouting that I was missing something."

"I wasn't shouting. I was just talking. I meant

the storm. Come and stand on the window frame."
She lifted him up. They were still three special and
equal friends, but the friendship had a most un-
comfortable, lopsided feeling. They counted the seconds between the flashes and the thunder, the interval
getting less and less until both happened together
and the house rattled its window frames. Then the
rain hurtled down, and they could see nothing more.

Ping believed that a promise is a promise, however small the person to whom it was made.

"Do you still want to go back to your nest, Oskar?
Because I promised I would take you. It would certainly be exciting in the orchard with the apples
flying like cannon balls and trees being struck and
the nest rocking under the gale. But the two outside
the nest would get very wet."

Oskar magnanimously agreed to wait till early
morning. "I'm hungry again," he said.

"I read that field mice have to eat every twenty
minutes or they die." Ida gave him some of her
medicinal girdle cake. It had a pleasant ship's-
biscuit taste.

The rain continued to sluice down the windows
and gurgle like brooks in the gutters. The thunder
circled round the outside of the sky, and the lightning lit up the room every few seconds but seemed
to have no further connection with any detonations.

The children were tired. Things had become more complicated than they had expected. Other adventures had not left them with a problem like Oskar's. The storm had sucked up and dashed away all their energy.

Ida punched a dent in Oskar's pillow and laid him in it, with enough girdle cake by him to last for the night.

"Don't play dolls with Oskar," said Ping. "It's horrid."

"I'm not playing dolls."

"You are. You're nearly as silly as Aunt Sybilla," said Oskar. "I'm fed up with your big hands."

This was the nearest to a quarrel that they had ever had.

They lay lonely and angry in their beds. And the rain teemed down and battered on the roof.

Ida had bad dreams. Out of Oskar's nest a huge hornet was crawling, its triangular face evil and satisfied. Then the lightning was the glint of cats' claws, striking and striking. She fought her way out of the sheets to a sitting position. She could hear Ping tossing in his bed, but not a sound from Oskar's. She felt for the switch and turned on the shaded lamp. Oskar was lying in bed, his hands under the back of his head, his long legs making a ridge down the middle, and his feet lifting up the blankets at the end. He turned his big gray eyes to Ida and smiled.

"I've just woken up too," he said. "Such a funny dream. Parts of it were lovely. But I got bored with it in the end, so I unthought it. Don't let's get up yet. I could do with hours more."

Ida stared at his blissful ordinariness.

"Wiggle your toes, Oskar."

"Idiot! Whatever for?" he answered, wiggling them.

"I just wanted to be sure." She put out the light with a deep sigh and turned back into dreamless sleep.

The River in Flood

By morning the sky had emptied itself and the river had filled to the brim and over. The children ran out after breakfast, determined to be first on the river and to get far away before the crowds came. Miss Bun had given them a picnic again, because the proposed visit of the committee had so filled her with hospitable ideas that her head was in a whirl. The day's outing therefore could be a long one and the children could go far afield.

When they reached the boat shed, the gangway was submerged, and the canoe, held by too short a mooring, was shipping water at the prow.

On windy days the surface of the river is raised in little pyramids streaked like the crisscross fork patterns on mashed potatoes. The children knew already that even a little wind can make a canoe tiresome to manage. Today, however, there was no wind. The surface looked like water just off the boil.

Inverted bowls of smooth water traveled along it with bubbles waltzing round them. The grasses rooted at the edge had no power to play at equal tug of war with the stream as they do on dawdling days. The children, however, were not experienced enough to know these as danger signs, and if there were no other boats out, they just thought they were successfully early. They held the canoe to the side, laughing as they mopped it dry because it tugged so impetuously. Then they got in and pushed off. Away it went downstream, broadside on. The children enjoyed the sensation of easy speed, thinking that the first lock would bring their joy ride to a safe, temporary stop. They managed after a struggle to keep the canoe straight, as was only proper. They might, Ida suggested, enjoying the adventurous thought, have to shoot a rapid. However, they kept well away from the weir, where the rapids were only too lifelike. They wanted to go as far down the main stream as possible.

When they came in sight of the lock, they were surprised to find both sides open and a heaped-up and purposeful swoop of water going straight through. They had no alternative but to swoop through also, holding their breath as the canoe struck the rough water on the other side. It shuddered, and the water battered under it as if it would stave in the bottom, whirling it sideways in a hopping motion, but the momentum carried it over. Almost before they realized they were safe, they were traveling rapidly down the lower reach.

"Isn't this fun!" said Ida. "We must be traveling faster than salmon. Would you think there could possibly have been so much water in the sky? I expect by this afternoon it will all be gone out to sea, and when we come back, the river will be just ordinary."

She underestimated the amount of water there can be in the sky. After a cloudburst the river goes on rising for many hours as the high ground nearer its source drains into it. Nor did she guess that, to prevent a flood, all the locks all the way to the sea were standing open to get the water away. Laughing and exhilarated, the three of them rushed along in their cockleshell.

Soon they had passed the island that hid Hermit Island. They thought of him fishing from his front door. They passed Owl Palace Island and were going farther than their farthest trip while the water stretched wider and wider on either side. None of the usual anglers were on the banks, for the reason that the banks had disappeared. They would have been fishing in the fields. For the same reason no one was out walking, or working. The swans, the wild duck, and the herons had the landscape to themselves. Where the current was swiftest the children rode along. The sun was now mercilessly out; the sides of the canoe burned their hands and knees. They passed through lock after lock, by small villages where cabin cruisers were moored fore and aft to the quays. A woman popped her head out of a cabin and shouted, "Are you all right?"

"Yes, of course," they replied, waving.

"Look out for the bridge!" cried a man. "Look out!"

Just in time the children lay back flat in the canoe as it went under a stone bridge with no head room. The flickering underwater-colored arch passed close over their faces, so that their eyes were obliged to focus on the grain of the stone, on the cracks and the lichen and the moss. It had a cold, secret smell, soothing on a hot day. On the far side of the bridge the land was less absolutely flat, with occasional patches of wood. They went through a long stretch with no houses at all, till they saw on a slope ahead of them, beyond a spread of flood water, a disused windmill. The proper course of the river took a right-angled bend in front of it.

"My arms are getting tired with trying to keep

the canoe straight," said Ida. "I don't want to wait till we get to the sea before I have lunch. Let's make for that windmill, straight over the bend."

It took the last ounce of their united strength to get out of the main current, even though it went close to the bend, but they made it, and there was enough water to float them, digging their paddles into the earth, over the bank and onto the quiet overspill.

It was a relief to be able to pause. Over the meadow the water was barely nine inches deep and the current negligible. They paddled softly toward the windmill, and now that the excitement was over, they chattered and laughed, and together with the quacking of the ducks that they disturbed, their voices were carried by the water to the far banks.

Ida was watching the butterflies that were traveling across all this water where there was no place to land—except on her upended paddle, where two stopped to rest. Ping's eyes were shut. He was sunning, smiling, and thinking his thoughts.

Oskar spoke in a tense voice.

"Look, you two. I haven't gone small again, have I?"

Ida and Ping turned their heads. "Not unless we have too," Ping answered.

"Then look in front. There, on the bank."

Ida looked toward the windmill. She had been facing it all the time, but had been more interested in what was round her—water rats swimming in search of land, earwigs troubled at finding themselves afloat on sticks. Now she searched the hillock where the windmill stood for something unusual. She saw nothing except a dead tree lying uprooted near the water's edge. Its roots had been broken off, all but two, and these were bent back under one of those fuzzy knobs that the boles of elm trees often have, which, if the tree had been a piece of sculpture, would have been the head of a reclining figure. There were only two branches left, and they were crossed one over the other like legs. Quite an ordinary thing to see, really. Only while she was looking at it, the branches moved and crossed the other leg over. And the foot swung contentedly in the lazy noon air.

Ping paddled the canoe nearer with all the strength of his silky melon-colored back, and as the three voices sharpened into exclamations, the swinging foot froze into immobility.

They grounded the boat and walked abreast through the shallow water, silent now except for the splash of their paddling.

The foot did not move again, but Ida, taking her eyes off it for a split second to look toward the

windmill, saw behind the broken windowpane a watching eye as big and bloodshot as a bull's.

Another eye as big, but clear, bright, and inquisitive, now opened in what Ida had once stupidly taken for a knob of a tree.

"Good morning, giant," said Ping, bowing.

The giant sat up. He was brown and tousled, but except for his size, they would have supposed him to be about fifteen years old.

"You weren't taken in, then," he said amiably.

"It was Oskar," said Ida. "This is Oskar. I would

have walked past you without thinking. And this is Ping."

"It's good to be noticed, for a change. I sometimes wonder whether people aren't going blind, or perhaps can't see anything bigger than themselves, like ants. I see them rushing about, but they never seem to look higher than their own shoulders. Except boys. Boys are always best." (Ida was ashamed.) "Babies, of course, they gaze up out of their prams with round eyes, willing to see anything that comes. I can even poke them and make them gurgle, but nobody takes any notice of what babies are looking at. Otherwise cats are the only things I have to talk to. They don't seem to notice any difference. Dogs always bark at me. They are a nuisance when I'm out foraging. But I manage. There's everything you could want in sheds and yards. They lock the gates, but I just reach over the top or put my arm through the skylight."

"Do you just take what you want?"

"What else could I do? Mother keeps saying I'll get caught and put in a cage, but it doesn't make sense. Anyway, if there's a commotion because somebody's missed a pig or a sack of potatoes, I just lean against a wall with a poster and everybody thinks I'm an advertisement. Or I lie down by the side of the road and they think I'm a new water main wrapped in sacking. Or I go on all fours behind a hedge and they think my backside is a horse. It's easy. Once I accidentally put my hand into some porridgy stuff that builders were using and left a print there. It was a very convenient place where I had taken a lot of different things. Afterwards I watched them holding a council round the print of my hand. The constable was there, and he got very angry about it. So did all the others. It wasn't a hand, he said, because it couldn't be, and he was not going to report it. What did they take him for? And all the time I was being part of a chestnut tree, and he had propped his bicycle against my legs."

"That's what the hermit said," said Oskar. "What you don't notice isn't there."

"My mother won't believe me when I say people don't see me. It wasn't like that when she was young, she says. You should hear her."

"TERAK!"

From the windmill came a voice like a cow's cracked with too much mooing.

"Terak! You will be the death of me. Didn't I tell you to come in?"

"That's Mother."

She came out, dropping to all fours in order to squeeze out at the double door. Her body was about as big as an elephant's and as shapeless and sloppy. She lumbered erect onto her legs, helping herself up by pushing with her hands on her knees. The many creases of her huge bony face showed a life-long discontent. There was not among them a line to show that she had ever smiled.

"Oh, my lumbago! What have you gone and done now, you good-for-nothing boy! They'll be after us. We'll have to move along again. And where will we go now, I'd like to know? In this miserable country we show up like pyramids. There's never a forest or a hill one can walk behind. Hardly as much as a haystack. All flat enough to break your heart. And the further east we go, the worse it is. And just when we were settled in this nice windmill, you've got to go and be seen."

"Why have you got to move? We won't tell anyone." Oskar was always the first to promise silence.

"Because I won't have my boy laughed at, that's why," she said with sudden ferocity. "I won't have it. He's like his father, growing as big as he can just to be annoying. But he's my boy and I won't have him laughed at. Dratted children! They're like water and lovers, get in anywhere. And their tongues will wag. Why didn't you do as you were told?" she went on, aiming a cuff at Terak, who easily dodged it. "You'll come to a bad end like your poor father.

The same one. I'm warning you. Now keep an eye on those children and don't let them escape. I don't know what I couldn't do to you for this. When I've put our things together, you can stow them in the canoe and pull it after you. The children will just have to stay here till the water goes down, and by then we'll have got clear." She heaved a sigh that scattered the straw on the ground like the flap of a blanket. "I wish I could lay my old bones down in my family cave. Blue and amber stony mountains they are there, with our own goats cropping and bleating among the boulders. But your poor silly father must want to be a great king! And his son's as silly as himself. Ah me, the bigger the woman, the bigger the burden laid on her. Watch those children now, Terak, or they'll be off like mice!"

She trundled away, dropping to all fours again to squeeze back into the mill. With amazement the children watched the bulk of her seat and the soles of her feet in the last heave before she disappeared. Across the back of her coarse blanket skirt the words *British Railways* were stenciled in white.

Terak sat crestfallen and dejected. All the animation of his face had drained away, and it looked as lifeless as a water butt.

Ida, Oskar, and Ping stood round him sympathetically, not knowing what to say. It was clear they had brought on a real calamity. For themselves, it was going to be difficult at home to explain the loss of the canoe, but it would be easier to get back without it, since they couldn't hope to paddle against the current. They would have to find a road and hitchhike in any case. For the moment, they were only troubled by the fabulous gloom of Terak's expression.

The silence lasted unhappily, until it seemed that no one would ever speak again. Terak sat unmoving like a great sad lump of tree. Then from inside the windmill came a gusty sound that was like a mixture of rookery, pigsty, and donkey farm. It snuffled and groaned and squealed and brayed in a long monody.

Terak came to life. He winked lovingly at Ping and uncovered his teeth in a smile. They were as big as matchboxes and whiter than the whites of his eyes. He nudged with his head in the direction of the mill.

"That's Mother playing her bagpipes. She always does that when she's upset. When she has used up all her puff, she'll go to sleep. So we have plenty of time to talk."

The three children sat down in a ring in front of him.

"What happened to your father?" was Oskar's first question.

"Where were the blue and amber mountains with caves and goats?" was Ida's.

"If your father wanted to be a king, was there a horse big enough for him to ride on?"

All three questions happened together, while Terak cupped both his ears with his hands. There was a silence after this traffic jam; then Ida began again.

"How old are you, Terak?"

"Mother thinks about a hundred and fifty. She notches the years on her walking stick, but some of the notches have worn off. You needn't look so unbelieving. Giants live longer than you do. Mother thinks she is five hundred, but she says she is very old for her age. She says she's worn out with trouble. She's melancholy company."

"Tell us all about everything, from the beginning."

"I don't know the beginning, except what Mother has told me. I don't remember my father. But Mother talks all the time, sometimes to herself, sometimes to me. She can't stop. Perhaps if she wasn't talking, she wouldn't believe in herself. I don't know where the mountains were. Somewhere in the east. They were very high, with such cliffs all round that nobody could get up or down. The giants lived on top. They had big caves with carved doorways along the side of a valley with a little stream. They kept goats and wove cloth and read the stars and worshiped the moon. They made music by hitting tall stones with wooden hammers. That was religious music for full moon. The bagpipes were only woman's music for funerals and sickness.

"One day, after an earthquake, my father found a place where rocks had fallen, where he could scramble down to the lowlands. He took my mother with him because they were courting and he wanted to show off. They went a long way for the pleasure of exploring. There were things they had never seen before, forests and flowers and animals, and a great river. All the time my mother kept on saying, 'We ought to go back now,' but my father would not. Then, coming out of a forest on a hillside, they startled some shepherds. These were the first little men they had seen, and of course my father was very interested and spoke kindly to them. But they ran away, leaving their sheep behind. So my father and mother became shepherds, and stayed there because it was spring and a lovely hillside. My father heaved up rocks and made a house, but my mother was homesick because she had left all her crocks and blankets in the cave. So he made her the bagpipes.

"One day when my father was watching the sheep and looking down over the valley, he saw a procession of little men on horseback, leading pack animals laden with bundles and a long covered wagon drawn by six horses. The little shepherds were with them, pointing up the hillside to him where he sat. Six of the riders came up the hill toward him. Some of them were fair-haired with faces colored like sandstone, but most were dark like the shepherds. When they came near enough, they shouted wonderful words, and bowed down, and waved flags. My father did not understand their language, but he sat still and made them a sign to come on. My mother was a good way off, in the house, playing the bagpipes because she wanted to go home.

"The men came near. They had brought presents, which they laid on the ground, an embroidered cloak, a turban with a peacock's feather sticking up at the front, a box of big blue beads, a dish of dates and figs and another of sweetmeats, and a bottle that the white man offered with a long speech and a specially low bow.

"When they saw that my father did not understand them, nor their interpreters either, they began to act in dumb show. Two of them placed the cloak and the turban on my father. They could reach because he was still sitting on the ground, leaning on one elbow to watch their antics. He liked the turban and the peacock feather, and when they started beating their foreheads on the ground and then waving their hands toward the waiting horsemen below in the valley, he understood that they wanted him to come and be their king. He let out a bellow for my mother, and it made the men turn and run. They couldn't help themselves. But the white man called them back. When they saw my mother—she was in her prime then with a face and figure like the Sphinx, so she says—coming down the hill, the men sat down plonk, like so many babies bumping on their bottoms.

" 'What's that tomfoolery?' she asked my father, pointing at his turban. He told her they wanted him to be king.

" 'King of that miserable little lot?' she said. 'Don't be such a fool.' But she sat down and tried the sweetmeats, and my father out of curiosity tried the bottle. It made him sneeze, but he liked it and came back for more. And my mother put on the blue beads. She wanted the turban then, but my father wouldn't let her have it. In the end they went with the men, who were very polite, bowing and scraping and flattering, serving up more and more food and drink, and making signs that it was proper kings and queens should be fat.

"But of course it was all a cruel hoax. They kept on luring my father toward his kingdom. He liked them less the more he saw of them, and my mother soon saw through it. They crossed the sea in a miserable ship with horses, elephants, tigers, lions, and monkeys and arrived in the end at a place called Bristol. By that time my parents were learning English. My mother was very quick. Soon she could understand what they said to each other as well as what they said to her. My father was a simple, easy man. He believed everything he was told. When they explained to him what he was to wear and do to be a proper king at his public acclamation, he learned it all very carefully. It was to take place in a very big green and yellow tent. They told him the ceremony had to take place for seven nights in every city of his kingdom. My father walked about very proudly, wearing his turban and peacock's feather, bowing and blowing kisses as he had been taught. He promised my mother they would go home again when it was all over, because kings and queens could do whatever they liked."

Terak paused for effect.

"But it was a circus, and they laughed at him."

He looked at Ida, Oskar, and Ping to see the result of this pronouncement. Their faces were keen and polite, but not struck wild-eyed with horror.

"My mother says it is the cruelest thing there is. He died of their laughter." Again he looked from one to the other, expecting groans.

"How?" asked Ping simply.

"It was this way. On the first night when everybody was screeching and laughing and the circus master had come on in his smart tight trousers and scarlet riding coat and cocked hat, and with his whip, my father lost his temper. He snatched the circus master up and put him across his knees and walloped him till the stool he was sitting on gave way. Then he chased the midget clowns with the whip, and they ran in every direction, tripping up and bolting between his legs. And the one he wanted most to beat ran up the ladder to the tightrope and took refuge on that. But he trod on the sausages dangling out of his pocket and slipped, hanging on to the rope with hands and knees. Then my father swarmed up the main tent pole and started along the tightrope too angry to think, and everybody shrieked with laughter still. And the rope broke and my father fell and broke his neck. But the clown clung to his end of the rope and swung down safely, and it looked as if he was climbing down his sausages. But when my poor mother ran in with her bagpipes under her arm—for she was afraid of losing them—and saw that he was dead, she was so heartbroken, she sat down in the middle and played the bagpipes most desolately. And the crowds laughed more and more. Then the clowns ran back and cleared everything away, including the carpet and father, and the next thing was the lions and lion tamer. While they were in the ring, my mother took me and ran away. She crossed the river at low tide and went and hid in the green mountains, where there were sheep. We lived there in a real cave. We have been hiding ever since, because it is a very dreadful thing to be laughed at—very dreadful indeed. Sometimes I try to imagine it when Mother has been scolding me. But I can't imagine it dreadful enough."

"What did your father have to do in the ring that made him suddenly so angry?" asked Ping.

"He came in blowing kisses to the people and called for the royal barber to shave him for his coronation. Crowds of midget clowns ran before him and after him, getting under his feet, spreading red carpets for him that they pulled away just as he stepped on them, and doing a great many rude things that only happen in circuses. For instance, a midget clown came in pulling a giant chamber pot along after him by a rope. That was very rude. But they called him Majesty all the time, and when at last he was seated on his throne, the barber came. He was the smallest of the clowns and the one my father hated most. He wore a white apron and had his hair curled like a baby's topknot, with a comb stuck in it. He had a pair of hedge clippers to cut my father's hair. Of course he couldn't reach, so he went trotting off on his busy little legs to fetch a stepladder, but that was still not high enough. It only came to my father's chest. So the clown could not reach his head, but he cut the hair on my father's chest instead, like someone clipping grass."

At this point Ping opened his mouth and let out a charming sound rather like the notes of a chaffinch.

Terak looked at him in astonishment.

"What was that?" he said. "What were you doing?"

The children were frightened and sorry. They all wanted to laugh, but held tight and said nothing.

"It was nice," said Terak. "Do it again, Ping." He grinned in expectation.

Then Ping laughed again, and the others could not help it. They laughed too. Terak gave a couple of hics like someone who does not know what comes next.

"I'm afraid we're laughing," said Ida, wiping her eyes. "I'm awfully sorry."

"Laughing? But it didn't hurt me at all. It was nice."

"Yes," said Oskar, wiping his eyes too.

"*Laughing!* Is that all it is?" And Terak began to laugh too, wildly, with more breath than he had got. "Oh! Oh!" he cried, clutching his ribs. "It hurts now. Oh! Oh! I shall die of it. Ooooh." He sat up at last and fetched out a handkerchief to wipe his eyes.

"Well I never," he said. "Fancy that. Let's do it again."

"Something has to be funny first," said Ping. Terak looked at him with adoration.

"I think I'd like to be a clown," he said.

Ida picked something out of the grass.

"This rolled out of your pocket when you pulled out your handkerchief. What is it? It looks like an ivory carving of four women."

"Oh, that! It's my tooth. I had toothache and Mother pulled it out. She tied it by a string to the lowest sail of the windmill. Then she took hold of the highest sail and jerked that down. It was easy. Would you like it for a keepsake, Ping?"

Ping accepted it with proper courtesy, but before he had finished his sentence, Terak, who was kneeling, bent forward and hid his face and hands in the grass, turning himself into a mere mound that could be sacks of carrots, or compost, or whatever one expects to see in the country. And the reason for this maneuver came into sight. A large and businesslike launch painted with official letters and numbers bore down the middle of the stream. Several men were on board, looking very alert with field glasses and a megaphone and a life buoy tied to coils of rope. They spotted the canoe first with great excitement, and then the children. The skipper bawled. "Hullo there!" through the megaphone, a magnified intrusion most unwelcome to the children.

"Hullo there! Are you all right?"

"Yes, thank you." Their voices sounded as squeaky as young swallows by contrast, and they waved out of politeness.

"Is the canoe damaged?"

"No, thank you."

But already two men were climbing overboard in thigh waders and splashing across the flooded field.

"I suppose you're the lot we're looking for," one of them said as they drew nearer. "Three kids in a canoe who shot under the bridge at Wigglesoke at about twelve o'clock? We're the search party," he added with a grin. "Lucky you didn't get out into the Wash. Tide's running out strongly there. What a trio of innocents! Didn't you know any better than that? However, it looks as though we shan't need you, doctor," he said to his companion. "Unless it's to certify them as idiots. Come on now. We'll give you a lift home and tow the canoe. Where do you come from?"

"Green Knowe, near Penny Sokey."

"It'll take us longer to get back than it took you to come. We'll telephone from the first pub and tell your people what we think of you."

The children were in a confusion of mixed feelings. They were abashed at being thought so silly; they were delighted at the prospect of the launch, and unwilling to leave Terak, especially without saying good-bye. Ping solved this difficulty by running over Terak's back from collar to seat and jumping down over his heels, as any child does to any challenging mound or boulder. Ida and Oskar followed, and the two men saw nothing but children behaving like children.

"Get in," they said, and towed the canoe by its mooring rope to the great humiliation of the three sitting in it. "Don't want you carried off downstream again." As they neared the launch, which was moored to a tree by the main channel, the children looked back for a last glimpse of Terak. There he was, boldly visible, cupping his hands round his mouth to shout, "I'm going to be a clown."

"Listen to that cow," said the skipper. "In the worst floods, I've known them to get stuck in trees. But judging by the noise, I should think that one's only separated from its herd. They're like women— can't bear to be alone."

When the children were pulled on board the launch, they thought of nothing but the glory and power of the return journey, perched up on the top deck and moving, with all the vigor of the engine beneath them, steadily upstream. They bit into their sandwiches with happy teeth, and the men made them hot cocoa and teased them about their reckless canoemanship in a way that left them feeling they were not too bad.

They took a much longer route because the launch could not pass under the stone bridge at Wigglesoke. When they arrived home, Miss Sybilla was certainly flustered, but it was difficult to tell whether it was because it had been given out on the one o'clock news that three children were at large on the flood, or whether it was because for some reason the cream would not whip up. Maud Biggin was not upset at all.

"Hullo, Ham, Shem, and Japhet!" was all she said, and thanked the rescue party politely but casually, as if they had brought back the cat.

"Children have nine lives," she said, "and if

Ida takes after her aunt, she's got ten." Even when the men told her that she would receive a bill later for the expenses of the rescue party, she only said, "Well, all experience has to be paid for, and a triple funeral would have cost much more."

"Maud! How can you say such things!" Miss Sybilla twisted the string of her melon beads round her hands, so that it broke and all the pips shot down inside her clothes. "Oh!" she said, hurrying out of the room.

Dr. Maud grinned at Ida. "I hope your voyage of discovery discovered something. They don't always, you know."

Ida felt at that moment particularly fond of her aunt. It was dreadful not to be able to tell her that they had discovered what would interest her more than anything else on earth. She opened her mouth and shut it again tightly. Oskar had promised silence for all of them.

"Come on, don't look so miserable, all of you," Dr. Maud went on. "I should have thought you'd had a first-class adventure and nobody any the worse."

Dr. Biggin Finds a Giant's Tooth

Up in the attic the children faced each other guiltily.

"It does seem a shame not to tell her. I'm sure she dreams about giants every night," said Ida. "If the committee gave her some money, she could take Terak's mother back to her mountains and be shown the caves and the giants still living in them."

"I promised," said Oskar. "And a promise to a displaced person is the most solemn promise of all."

"But Terak's mother wants to go back."

"You don't understand," said Ping. "They don't send displaced persons home. They put them in camps. They might even put them in the zoo."

"Without telling Aunt Maud anything about Terak, couldn't we show her the tooth? It would prove one giant."

"She'd enjoy it much more if she found it herself," said Ping. "And we wouldn't have to tell any lies. Where could we put it for her to find?"

"On the gravel path where she always walks up and down thinking out her book."

"Yes! Since the new gravel was spread there, she can't take her eyes off it. She is always hoping, I don't know what for. She must find the tooth before the meeting tomorrow; then she can tell them all."

Three pairs of sand shoes pattered and skipped down the steep wooden staircase, only noticed by Dr. Biggin as a sound of gaiety and by Sybilla Bun as a sound of healthy appetites.

The children crossed the garden as if they were going to mark the fall of the floods. They drew a deep line in blue pencil on the bark of an ash tree at water level. Anybody could see their only interest was the river. On the way back along the gravel path, Ping stooped to pick up a woolly bear caterpillar, and the tooth was planted. Anybody could see that he had found something that interested three naturalists. They withdrew to their attic, and there two went on with the map while the other kept watch at the window. The full length of the roll of lining paper was not enough for their day's travel. They could only put an arrow with the direction, "To Terak's Windmill."

"Is she there yet?" the artists on their knees on the floor asked from time to time.

"No, not yet. She ought to have a lot to think

about for tomorrow. Why doesn't she come? Bother, here's a caller. What shall we do if someone else picks it up first?"

The caller, however, went along the path looking only at the house, noticing its arklike shape and the cluster of heads like the monkeys usually painted on the attic windows of Noah's arks. He asked for Mrs. Oldknow, to whom the house belonged, but she of course was away. Very soon the children saw him retrace his steps, looking to left and right, but never on the ground. The iron gate clicked as he latched it, and his footfalls along the river path made a kind of clock to tick-tock away at least five minutes of the children's suspense. Soon the gate clicked again. Seldom, they thought, had the little gravel path had so much traffic. This time it was a neighbor come to ask if the children who had been lost were all right. With anguish they saw her stop halfway down the path and stoop to the ground. It was only to retie a loose shoelace, and on she went, thinking perhaps of washing machines.

"She pushed it with her toe," said Ping. "After all, it's big. I can see it from here."

"Perhaps it's too big to be seen," said Oskar, "like Terak himself. Perhaps you should have buried it so that only one prong stuck out."

"Too late now. Here she comes."

Dr. Maud Biggin came out to take the air. As usual, she walked along the gravel path, bending forward, her hands clasped behind her, humming a tuneless sound and shuffling the loose surface absent-mindedly as she paused to undo a knot of thought. Sometimes she even, surprisingly for a woman of her age, dribbled one of the rounder stones in little kicks before her for the length of the path. After passing over the tooth no less than six times while the children held their breath and tried to will her to see it, Dr. Maud at the seventh time kicked it sharply. It did not roll, but sprang and turned somersaults as if determined with its four molar legs to attract her attention with odd acrobatics. She merely followed it up and kicked it again.

Ida groaned. "She must be thinking horribly hard. Suppose she kicks it into the river."

But at the gate Dr. Maud turned as usual and, still spasmodically sending the tooth before her, advanced toward the house. The children, forgetting that they must not seem to expect anything, stood at the open window above her. Ping's face was inscrutable. Ida was trembling, and Oskar had his fiercest willpower stare. Dr. Maud suffered a sort of spasm of thought. She unlocked her hands from behind her, slapped at the midges on her arms and legs, and as if something was now quite clear in her mind, set off at twice the pace toward the house and her desk. As she came to the tooth lying where she had kicked it, she as good as passed it—then stopped dead, frozen in the bent position that was habitual to her, and stared at it.

"Eh! What! No!" she ejaculated, picking it up and turning it over. She wiped her spectacles and looked at it again. Her hand trembled. "No!" The children had the reward of seeing her look as surprised as people are supposed to look on arriving in heaven.

A little later, when they and Miss Sybilla were

ready for supper, Dr. Maud came in wearing the crash helmet that sat so incongruously on her studious head. She looked purposeful and secretive, almost guilty.

"Maud! It's suppertime. Where are you going?"

"Sorry, Sybilla. Something has turned up—umhum, umhum, has come to my notice—that I must have Dr. Oldmolar's advice about before tomorrow. Very odd. Very odd indeed. Very interesting. I wish there was more time before the meeting to examine the situation. No time for supper." Off she went, hurrying as if she had nearly tripped and had to catch up with her balance. The silent supper party heard her motorcycle kicked into action and pop-popping away down the drive.

At breakfast next morning, which was the day of the great meeting, Dr. Maud was almost unrecognizable with excitement. Her eyes darted here and there, and she looked ready to defy the world. So distant were her thoughts that she ate as people eat alone, with a bulging cheek and uninhibited swallowing noises, until Miss Sybilla said, "Maud! Maud, dear! What are you thinking of today! You are not yourself."

"Ten times myself today, Sybilla. Today I'm going to make archaeological history. Today I'm going to throw a bomb that will rock the Society." She pushed away her unfinished plate.

"Maud, dear! Eat your grilled tomatoes while they are hot. They cool in a minute."

"Grilled tomatoes! Is that all you can think about? Look at the children." She looked from one to the other and met three pairs of eyes fixed on her with brilliant expectation and sympathy. "Look at the children—even they realize that some things are important. Ida! Are you taking your paradurra Abyssiniensis regularly?"

"Yes, Aunt Maud."

"Good girl. Now help Sybilla to carry the chairs and get things ready, and then make yourselves scarce."

The river had gone down better than could have been expected in one night. It was back within its banks, running strongly but without those wanton waltzing dimples that the children knew now as danger signals. The canoe had been left at a boatbuilder's on the way home yesterday because it had sprung a leak in being dragged across a submerged strand of barbed wire at the edge of Terak's meadow. The boatbuilder had rented them a punt until the canoe could be repaired. After the light balance of the canoe, it seemed as steady as a liner.

Holidaymakers in launches were venturing out again. The riverbank was thick with people carrying picnic baskets and wireless sets. The children decided to go to the mill pool and from there explore a mere crack of a waterway that could only float a boat when the water was high.

The little tributary seeped between an avenue of bulrushes, whose handsome chocolate maces bowed to them as the ripple that the punt pushed before it reached their stalks and set them in motion. Ping said he felt like a mandarin approaching his palace. But it was not a palace that they came upon, but a second and totally secluded pool on whose circumference three little weirs tinkled like musical boxes. Their waters lost themselves in the bulrushes, which quickly hushed them, leaving the central expanse still.

The delighted children stopped paddling, and every crease faded off the surface. The punt lay as if on a mirror, which itself lay in empty space, for above and beyond the frame of bulrushes they could see nothing at all. There were white clouds above them and white clouds below, floating in a complete orb of hyacinth blue. When the swallows dipped to catch a fly, they disputed each fly with the swallow that came up to meet them from below. The flies themselves in alighting on the surface met foot to

foot with their doubles. Even an ice-cream carton
alone in the blue space had a twin soul leaning
toward it with the same enticing words in pink written upside down. And all the doubles were mysterious, both more shadowy and more brilliant than
the originals because of an azure varnish that alone
distinguished them. Ping lay over the end of the
punt with his arms in the water up to the elbows

and considered the black and golden Ping that considered him. Ida was twiddling above the surface with her fingers as if they were mosquito legs to watch the precision with which the other fingers came to touch them. Oskar was standing, tall and sunburned, and the other Oskar stuck down into the water exact and beautiful.

"It makes me wonder which is you," said Ida.

"This one and I are sharing arms," said Ping. "He's got me up to the elbow and I've got him, like Siamese twins."

Oskar said, "It's only if we stay above the water that there are two. If I were to dive in, I should slip right inside him and there would only be one. Doesn't that prove that the one underneath is the real one and I'm only a sort of water ghost? I'm going to try."

He neatly dived in, and Ida saw the two Oskars meet and fuse till there was only one swimming away underwater. She was surprised how wretched she felt. "I wish he would come up again," she said, looking anxiously all around. Oskar's head bobbed up some distance away.

"There he is," said Ping. "Unless it's only a water ghost coming up to climb in the punt with us!"

"Let's all be water ghosts then, in case," said Ida, and in they flashed.

When, after struggling up over the side with elbows bent up like grasshoppers' legs, they were all in the punt again and getting their breath, Oskar said, "I was right, you see. That was the real one."

"Which are you now, then?"

"I still feel the real one."

"Then what's the one that's in the water now, underneath you?"

"Oh, I expect that's just the one that thought he was me."

"We shall get horribly mixed up," said Ida, diving in again. When she came up, she turned on her back and floated among the reflected clouds. The sun beat on her eyelids, which looked to her crimson like pieces of stained glass.

They never had a more delicious day. There was no sound except the splash of their dives and the drip off their hair and elbows as they sat in the punt, and their own happy nonsense. The pool was a world as much their own as their most private thoughts. Ida's nicest dreams for a long time afterward were ringed with a palisade of swinging bulrushes.

Toward the end of the afternoon she saw Oskar, who had gone exploring, standing among the bul-rushes with something in his arms. "Bring the punt," he shouted. "I've got something here I don't want to drop." Ida paddled across to him, and he climbed in with his treasure. "I found it bedded in the rushes." He was hugging a green glass bottle. It was thick and balloon-shaped with a long neck and a rim at the mouth. It had a cork tied with wire and covered with sealing wax. It was not heavy enough to be full, but it had something inside.

"It was bedded in the rushes and all grown over. I trod on it by mistake, and it went right down in the mud. I expect it came down once in a flood and was left in the rushes when the water went down. Isn't it a splendid shape?" Nobody had a corkscrew to open it. They must wait till they got home.

As they approached Green Knowe, they saw crowds of people stopping to look over the garden wall with amused curiosity. The drive was full of cars belonging to the archaeologists attending Dr. Biggin's meeting, which was taking place indoors behind wide-open windows. Miss Sybilla Bun was standing outside with an expression of deep but muddled distress, lacing her fingers into her beads as if trying to tell half a dozen rosaries at once. She was eavesdropping, if it can be called that when people have forgotten everything but their desire to make themselves heard, for the meeting was in an uproar. The sounds that came across the garden were surprising in the extreme, as if only the most preposterous voices could force their way out from the angry buzz inside.

Ida, Oskar, and Ping were less squeamish than Miss Sybilla. They dropped their picnic baskets and ran to the open windows to satisfy their curiosity.

Nearly all the guests were standing up, very red in the face. The chairman was shouting "Order! Order!" and banging the table with one hand while with the other he pushed his white hair on end, leaving his spectacles mislaid and useless on top. Some members were shouting at him, some at each other, some simply into the air, which was already so full of noise it couldn't absorb any more. "I protest!" "Shame!" "Sit down!" "Outrage to the dignity of . . ." "Impudent fake!" "A plastic advertisement for the forthcoming dental conference!" "All the more shocking because of the previous honorable record . . ." "An insult to our revered chairman!" One gentleman, lifting his hand in a gesture of deep shock, accidentally knocked off the pince-nez of another, and for a moment or two they snarled at each other like a couple of fox terriers. Another crumpling his sheaf of papers into a ball hurled it down in front of the chairman, shouting, "I resign!" and elbowed his way out of the room.

All this time Dr. Maud Biggin stood her ground

and continued to make herself heard when she could. "This most startling piece of evidence . . . bewildering and stimulating lines of thought . . . no time as yet to submit laboratory tests . . . the necessity of an immediate charter to explore the gravel fields . . . probable proof on our own doorstep . . . duty of facing up to truth however unlikely . . ." and so on. She was sorrowful but undaunted, and perfectly even-tempered under abuse. When, however, somebody pushed up opposite her and bawled, "I accuse Dr. Maud Biggin of fraud," she replied almost casually, "You're a silly old fool," and sat down.

The three children applauded vigorously from the window sill. The committee appeared to notice them for the first time and even to see themselves as others saw them. The noise died down while the chairman announced sternly that the meeting was adjourned indefinitely. He then made his way out, stopping to apologize to Dr. Biggin for his inability to keep order. "Scientific passion ran very high, dear lady, very high indeed." The others put themselves and their papers in order and followed him out. Some marched past their hostess with a harsh inclination of the head; some shook hands and apologized for "bad behavior in some quarters" as if their own had been any better. Old Harry put a wax-white hand on her shoulder and, after moving his thin wolfish lips in and out, said, "I would like it, Maud. I would like it very much. But it won't do. Pity! It's just a little ahead of the evidence."

"Evidence! This is the evidence," she retorted, angry at last, shaking Terak's tooth under his nose. *"It's a giant's tooth.* All we need now is to find the gravel bed that it came out of and fix the date. Admittedly, I don't understand its almost perfect preservation, but analysis of the site will perhaps explain that."

Old Harry shook his head and patted her shoulder again. "A pity, Maud. A great pity. But you took it very well."

Dr. Maud turned to the three children who were looking on all this time with profound sympathy and indignation. She winked at them.

"Ever heard the proverb, 'There's none so blind as those that won't see?' Anyway, I called one of them a silly old fool, didn't I? There's no pleasure like letting rip."

Meanwhile, the departing guests, ashamed of their behavior to one hostess, were thanking Miss Sybilla with extra warmth for her kindness and the most delicious luncheon. Really exquisite. They smiled. "We shall never forget it." So Miss Sybilla came in and said, "There! After all, Maud, it went off very well, I think. I think they all enjoyed it. Perhaps just a little indigestion in the afternoon. The lobster was very rich. But it passed off."

The green bottle was taken upstairs to be opened in private.

"It has been thrown out of a ship in the middle of the ocean, I expect," said Ida, "with a farewell message inside from the last survivor. But I can't think how it got here. The tide couldn't bring it up so far from the coast."

"Perhaps it could sail upstream before a strong east wind."

"It would have to go through hundreds of locks." Ida jerked the word "locks" very loud, because at that moment the cork came free. "It is a message. I knew it would be." She pulled out a roll of parchment, kneeling on the floor to spread it out. It had been rolled up for so long that it shot back like a roller blind. It took all three of them to hold it flat. It was closely written in a difficult handwriting. The paper was headed with an ink drawing and a title. The picture showed the silhouette of a tall house in a clearing among big trees. A full moon appeared to rest on the point of the roof. The title read, "The Island of the Throning Moon."

They all read it aloud with different degrees of excitement and disbelief in their voices.

"He was marooned on an island," said Ida. But Ping pointed with his slim finger.

"I think that house is this house." And so it could have been.

After a gasping moment Ida's brain began to work again.

"One of these islands round here must be called the Island of the Throning Moon. And it must be somewhere opposite this house so that when the moon is full, it looks like that from there."

"We'll have to go by moonlight, then," said Oskar.

"A yellow moon, like a Chinese lantern," said Ping lovingly.

"Now let's try to read what it says."

"This is the Confession of Piers Madely, Vicar of the Parish of Penny Sokey, written in the year of Our Lord 1647. It has been my Misfortune to undergo an Experience so far outside the Logic that should rule civilized Thought, that the whole Fabric of my Mind is suffering Strain therefrom. Inasmuch as I cannot disburthen myself of this Matter to any living Soul, neither to my Lord Bishop nor to any of my Parishioners learned or simple, for fear that they, being unable to believe me, should impute to me either Witchcraft or a Lunatic humour, Yet because of the Need that afflicts me to confide to some Human Being concerning that which I have seen, and been present at, I have devised to set it down in writing enclosed in a Bottle, entrusting it to the fearful Floods that now overwhelm the land, that they may carry my Confession away from here, and haply after many Days it may come into his hands who will give it Credence. And lest it fall into the hands of ignorant or malicious Persons during my Lifetime (which if such Trials continue cannot be long), I have writ it in Latin. Of which, though the Language may be faulty, for I have ever found Latin a difficult Tongue, being but an indifferent Scholar, yet every Word is true. And this I swear before the Almighty's awful Throne."

"Oh, blow!" said Ida. "All that and we can't read it."

"We can go and find out," said Ping in his little, remote voice.

"It's obviously something pretty awful."

"Demons"—Ping smiled deliciously—"by moonlight."

Ida was still thinking aloud. "Flying Horse Island is exactly opposite here. Surely he can't have been so frightened by *them*. I know they aren't supposed to be here, but wouldn't anybody think it a lovely secret to have? There's an island beyond that. Perhaps we could see the house from there. We will have to go anyway. The moon will be full tomorrow. We will watch what time it rises tonight, and tomorrow it will be forty minutes later."

The next day, very early in the morning when the moon was setting and it was queer enough for anything, they set off for the island lying north of Flying Horse, to find out whether Green Knowe could be seen from there. To their surprise it could not. It sank back into a belt of trees among which even the yews could not be distinguished. It was hard to believe that a house, which, when you were near it, cut into the sky so proudly and dominated the surroundings with the assurance of its stone-built corners, could from half a mile away efface itself completely. The children looked for it in vain.

"We are on the wrong track," said Ida. "If we can't see it by daylight, we certainly couldn't at night. But just *in case* the drawing is of Green Knowe, we will come out tonight and watch to see if the moon really does pass exactly over the gable point. Perhaps it doesn't at all. I can't imagine fearful things happening near Green Knowe. I know it is very old, but it feels like a refuge, something to be trusted."

"Green Knowe hasn't been there always," said

Oskar. "Perhaps whatever frightened poor Piers Madely was older than the house. Something so old that it didn't make sense, like the worst things in dreams."

They calculated that the moon should rise at eleven and might be over the house by midnight. There was a light in Maud Biggin's room when the children crept out. "She's still thinking about the tooth. She won't hear us."

Outside, had there been streetlights or headlights, you would have thought it was dark. There were massed shadows on the earth, but the sky was aware of the moon just under the horizon and was catching a reflection of its light and relaying it to the river. Seen from the punt, the world was a symmetrical but unfamiliar pattern of bulky blacknesses jutting onto quicksilver. The daylight line between reality and reflection was gone. All the shapes were equally black, equally dense, and hung like clouds whose position in space is unknown, so that it was only if the punt passed through it, instead of bumping on it, that a reflected shadow could be known as such. The water, that is as much of its surface as could be seen, wound among looming masses, which at one moment, if the children put out a hand to ward them off, were found not to be there, at another would be lowering, smothering, and catching on their hair. The course of the river that they thought they knew so well was as mysterious as a foreign language. They had to keep touching the surface with their paddles to reassure themselves that it was there, that they were on it, that it was the river they knew.

When at last the moon, heralded by a coppery haze, appeared above the flat earth and rolled behind the cottages like an immense orange beach ball, the enchantment was complete. Moonlight alone was a breathtaking adventure. The Amazon River could not have bettered it.

At its first coming the moon seemed almost to bounce up; its movement could be watched. But once properly in the sky, it hung like time. The children were so much under its spell that anything that might happen in its wild and ancient light could only seem in keeping. They were afraid only of missing the magic moment when the moon should sit throning on the point of their bedroom roof. They paddled up and down the homestretch, passing repeatedly.

"Of course!" said Ida suddenly. "Green Knowe itself is on an island! *It happens here*."

They moored the punt in their boathouse and stole back hesitantly on to the lawns, for once hand in hand. There was no denying that it looked very strange. When the sun is in the sky, every eye turns away to escape the blaze, but the moon compels sight and thought to follow its course up toward the zenith, with the result that by contrast the height of trees and buildings seems dwarfed. Green Knowe seemed smaller, but at the same time charged with awe. It had changed its friendly old fairy-tale quality for something far older and terrifyingly different. The house drew and held their attention, so that the transformation of the moonlight-flattened garden went unnoticed. The bone-white walls were streaked with shadow patterns of leaves that were rhythmic and interlacing like patterns left by the ebb tide on sands. It had a curious look of wickerwork, which the rippling unevenness of the roof repeated. By daylight Green Knowe looks planted on the earth deliberately for all time, but now the glimmering outline before them looked as if it grew out of the earth, lightly springing up. No windows showed, but the house had a kind of dim glow. If Ida allowed herself to think of the walls as woven of rushes, instead of stone-built three feet thick, then the hollow interior was so much the bigger and, having no upper floors, must be imagined, by the marvel of its being constructed at all, as a sort of cathedral.

"Doesn't it look queer?" said Ping. "Almost as if the moon shone through it!"

"It's built of rushes," said Oskar, as though that were not a matter for disbelief.

The moon was going up like a kite. She had cleared the trees and was moving above the slant of the roof, just short of the finial. A drift of silky cloud was moving along to meet her ascent. The children approached the apex of the shadow of the building where it lay across the ground. Quite suddenly the cold brilliance above and the darkness into which they were walking filled them with a sense of fear as limitless as the night. They all had the same thought—while their eyes had been mesmerized by the moon, *they had forgotten to watch out*. In that moment they became aware of a figure just in front of them, standing immobile at the point of the shadow and gazing up at the point of the house as they themselves had done a second before. The dark form was tall and roughly cloaked. It seemed to have a stag's head with antlers and long naked human legs. The children dropped to the ground and backed into the nearest clump of bushes, from which they looked out like foxes. In the unnatural silence they could hear each other's teeth chattering. It sounded loud enough to give them away, but they could not control it. It grew, as if in a nightmare the volume had been turned up. It seemed to shake the shadows and fill the open spaces, to materialize in figures that had

not been there and now were. They grew out of the milky darkness and showed as silhouettes with deer's horns, with skins flapping over their shoulders as they moved. Each carried a spear, which he shook high as he leaped repeatedly in salute to the moon, a wild homage that took place in absolute silence except for the unexplained rattling that increased as the leaping grew more furious. It had grown out of the chattering of their own teeth but was now something quite outside themselves and very threatening. Meanwhile, the leader, wearing the stag's antlers, remained motionless like an inspired sorcerer proud with power.

As the moon moved to her appointed throne and shone there resplendent and worshipable, the leader gave a long wolf howl and broke into a pantomime of dreadful activity. The horned crowd opened out into a ritual dance, stamping round him to the accompaniment of a rhythmic rattling that was continuous and unnerving. It suggested rudimentary instruments such as tambourines and "the bones." It suggested also pursuit and death and the rattle of dry reed beds. The movements and gestures of the dancers were only less frightful than those of the leader, who was a genius in horror. They had a dramatic but inexplicable compulsion. The white-faced children felt that their limbs twitched and stamped of their own accord, that they could not keep out of it. This lasted until the moon had passed over and was reigning, gloriously independent, in her sky. Then the dancers slipped the deerskins off their heads, wearing them like capes, and whirling round, they charged—as it seemed to the children— straight at them, as if they had only waited for the end of their ritual to take vengeance on the intruders. They came within a spear's length—but passed straight on, making for the riverbank. In that dreadful moment the children saw at close quarters the savage faces painted in black-and-white stripes, the hands painted red. They saw too, glinting in the cold light, the cause of that skeletal rattling, for every hunter wore round his neck strings of tusks, or horns, or teeth, which knocked together as they swung to his movements. It was not a sound that could travel far, but the chatter of dead teeth must have come as the first warning of danger to nervous ears waking out of sleep in the marshlands.

The hunters streamed by the children, almost jostling them, but as the leaders had passed them unnoticed, so did all the rest, like a herd of animals. They boarded canoes that, from the sound of it, were hidden in the rushes near at hand. Their rapid paddle strokes drove through the water, where the moor hens fled with loud midnight cries, and the wild duck wheeled into flight with half-breathed clucks of alarm.

The children cautiously parted the leaves and crept out from their hiding place. They looked down the river, hoping to see the craft with their standing crews. But the moon had now met the shoal of cloud and passed behind it, so that from one moment to the next everything became dim and shadowy. A cold shudder of wind blew on the back of their necks and ears, and rustled the balancing surface of blade and leaf along the river's edge and across the wide meadows. They were standing at midnight, alone, under a sky that was there before either earth or moon had been and would be there long after. In this agonizing second of revelation that ALL passes, the bark of a disturbed heron caused them to clutch each other, and jerked loose their tongues.

"Where can we go?" asked Ida. "Where is there for us to go to now?"

"I suppose we could just *look* in that—that wattle place," said Ping, for once hesitant.

"We've got the busman hermit for company," said Oskar. "He's been wherever this is, once. Or perhaps I should say 'whenever' this is. But I don't want to go on the river. It's too much. We are *really* displaced now." Yet they turned instinctively toward

the house—"That wattle place" as Ping called it—
because where else? Above its obscure silhouette
the cloud was outlined with silver on its upper edge,
where suddenly a dazzling diamond-white segment
appeared, and the moon came out. She dropped the
cloud from about her, and round and brilliant as a
singing note she hung in the center of the sky.

Under her lovely light Green Knowe was re-
vealed again, gentle, heavy, and dreaming, with its
carefully spaced bushes and trees standing in their
known positions enriched with moonlight on their
heads and shadows like the folds of Cinderella's ball
dress behind them.

The children gasped with joy and relief, and
slowly taking in, holding, and keeping what they
saw, they moved toward home. They all three slept
in one bed that night, because, as Oskar had said,
it was too much. As Ping wriggled himself into the
little space allotted to him between Ida and Oskar,
his last words were: "They had as many beads as
Miss Sybilla." And he laughed to himself.

"Aunt Maud," said Ida (by arrangement with the
others), as she helped herself to cereals, "have there
ever been wickerwork cathedrals? I mean, in the
Stone Age?" She spoke casually, as one might ask,
"Did they eat honey?"

Dr. Biggin put a spoonful in her mouth, while she turned over a page, and then answered rather mouthily, "There are some still, in places like Borneo and the Persian Gulf. Or were till the other day. Nowadays civilization moves so fast, you can't travel fast enough to keep up with it. The only thing anyone can say for certain is that it was there yesterday, if they haven't pulled it down since."

"Oh! Might they be as big as this house?"

"They couldn't be as big, but they might look it, because of being so much bigger than anything else around. They *look* the biggest house you can think of. And they are, because you couldn't possibly make anything bigger out of the material."

"Oh," said Ida again meekly. "Thank you."

"Do Stone Age people worship the moon?" she ventured again a little later on.

"Eh? How should I know! Very probably. Goddess of the chase and patroness of fishes."

Miss Sybilla burst unexpectedly into the discussion. Rattling her beads with excitement and looking rather pink, she recited:

> "Queen and huntress, chaste and fair,
>   Now the sun has gone to sleep,
>   Seated on thy silver chair
>   State in wonted splendor keep."

She smacked her lips.

Oskar and Ping looked at her as at an oracle. *"Seated on thy silver chair,"* repeated Ping softly. And Oskar continued, *"State in wonted splendor keep."*

Miss Sybilla blushed crimson at their appreciation. "Don't you know that poem, Ida?"

"Yes, Aunt Sybilla. It goes on about goddess *excellently bright*. I like it. Excellently bright sounds sharp, like scissors. As if the moon was cutting the sky."

"You've all been sleeping with the moon on your pillows," said Dr. Biggin. "You too, Sybilla. I never knew you were poetical."

"It was so romantic last night. It made me feel quite . . . what shall I say? Quite *wild*. I wanted to dance on the lawns."

Dr. Maud, for want of any other woman to wink at, winked at Ida. But the children were not laughing. They looked, with eyes full of questioning astonishment, at fat Sybilla Bun and her beads.

The Circus

It is not to be expected that every day of the holidays will be filled with such adventures. Ida, Oskar, and Ping were never at a loss and never bored. Many pleasant ordinary things can be done a second time, though they are never twice alike. The really extraordinary things can never be repeated.

One day, near the end of their time, Ping came back from the village, where he had been with Miss Sybilla to carry her basket for her to the bus stop. He had been away a long time, while Ida and Oskar had been kicking their heels, waiting to start out until he should come back. He was very excited and could not get his news told.

"What an age you have been," said Ida.

"I know. I've done a lot in the time. There's going to be a circus at Penny Sokey."

"Well, we shan't be here to go to it. Hurry up; it's our last day on the river."

Ping began again, refusing to budge even when pushed.

"I saw the posters in the shop. It begins tonight, so we could go. The posters say—Ida! You are not listening."

"You can tell us on the way," said Ida, walking off with Oskar full tilt toward the boathouse.

Ping caught up and danced along backward ahead of them to make them listen.

"It's exciting. It's important. The poster says:

GREAT NEW STAR TURN
TERAK THE GIANT."

"What!" Ida and Oskar plonked down everything they were carrying and stood stock-still.

"He's done it," said Ping. "He's a clown. We must take Dr. Biggin and let her see him. I have been helping at the shop, unloading a van full of boxes. That's why I was so long. I have got some money. They say they are short-handed, so if we all go back and help, we can make enough to invite Dr. Biggin to the circus as a thank-you. Then she will have to come."

Ping was quite right in his understanding of Dr. Biggin's mind. She was not very interested in circuses except as survivals—very degenerate of course—of circuses and games long past. But she appreciated gratitude, and as the children had invited her, she accepted. She was, besides, in a high good humor. Ida had been measured for the last time and had grown three-quarters of an inch. Miss Sybilla, of course, had said it had nothing to do with those silly old grass seeds. It was the good food the child had had and plenty of fresh air. The two ladies wrangled on the subject, with the result that Miss Sybilla had refused to come to the circus, giving as her reason that she couldn't bear to see a horrid man bullying the poor helpless tigers—which was a funny way of looking at it but quite true. Oskar understood. The tigers stood for his father, overpowered, imprisoned, and angry.

They hired a second canoe to take Ida and Dr. Biggin. She proved to be a powerful canoeist. As she paddled, she made wild noises, which she said she had heard savages do to keep the beat, on her voyages of exploration. Only, she said, they stood up to paddle. Oskar and Ping had been sitting in their canoe, because they thought it was to be a sedate, grown-up excursion. They now accepted the challenge and stood to paddle, for of course Ping had been practicing this too. Dr. Biggin urged them on with short barking shouts, and the two canoes raced neck and neck. It was a wonder Oskar and

Ping did not take a double header into the water. Dr. Biggin did not care whether they did or not, which is probably why it did not happen. They began to wish she had been with them on the river all the time. It was stimulating to be with someone who was always thinking of jungles or marshes, who when she shouted, "Paddle, boys!" might be addressing pigmies or South American Indians. They felt, guiltily, that they had underrated her company. Ping remembered the yellow cat that had been lying along a branch over their heads and that reminded him of a tiger. He felt that if Dr. Biggin had been with them, it would have been a real one.

However, after a while she roared out, "Take it easy, boys. I'm an old woman," and got out her cigarettes. Ida and the boys paddled along till they came to the wide water meadows. At the far end they could see the roof of the Big Top, surrounded by swings, tractors, trucks, and caravans of every sort.

Dr. Biggin, between puffs, said she liked tents. "I have no doubt tents go back nearly as far as wattle. As far behind my civilized giants as they are behind us. And that's a thought! Right back. And funny men too. As soon as there were three men, one of them was a funny man."

"Why are funny men always little?" said Ida,

who couldn't keep her mouth shut any longer. "What if one of them was a giant?" Three pairs of eyes met in an electric flicker of excitement, for Maud Biggin had as yet no idea what she was to see. She merely grunted at Ida's childishness, too foolish to need an answer. The children, however, were as pleased as if she had exclaimed, "I would give my eyes to see a giant just once." They knew she would soon grunt to a different tune.

As they drew nearer to the circus, a noise as savage and primitive as anyone could imagine traveled to meet them along the water. Several steam organs were playing different tunes of giant loudness. The din seemed to tear one ear away from the other. It was painful but intensely exciting. Mixed in with the strident, clashing tunes and the babel of men yelling the attractions of their swings or coconut shies were occasional angry jungle roars and sinister cat-fight snarls. Quietly detached from all this, walking in single file toward them across the meadow, was a man leading three elephants. The children thought they were coming for a drink and were delighted at getting a preview at close quarters. They paddled nearer to the elephants, but the keeper shouted and waved his arms, and Dr. Biggin rapped out, "Lay in to the far bank!" There they held on to the willow branches and watched while the elephants, squealing like pigs, took to the water, making, as they submerged their great bodies, waves that would have capsized the canoes. This, of course, was the best jungle scene the children had ever had, and their imaginations were so fired, they almost managed not to hear the din from the circus ground. The elephants lolled and rolled slowly about in the water all ways up. Sometimes nothing showed but the big rounds of their feet; sometimes the pointed domes of their foreheads or backs stuck up like rocks washed with muddy ripples, and disappeared again. Or the great island of their barrel sides divided the stream, with water running off all round as if off a hillside. Once quite near the canoe a snorkel trunk-end came up near Ida, fumbling in the air like a laughing mouth without a face, followed later by a flat wrinkled drift of side face, out of which a small humorous eye opened, saw her, winked, and submerged again, while the canoe rocked with the backwash of huge but soft displacement of water. When the keeper called, the elephants—like children who obey but only just— slowly drew to the bank, squirting their backs as they waded out, then rolling in the mud again so that they had to have a second wash. They set off then in single file back to their job, frisking their comic tails and vigorously swinging their trunks. By this time crowds of children were running up from the circus ground, some luckier than others with buns to offer, which the elephants took from their hands in passing with no sign of gratitude except the smile they sucked in with the bun.

In the distance a drum began booming while a man yelled into a megaphone, "Walk up, walk up."

They hurried downstream toward the mooring place, passing the caravans and trailers, among which Oskar noticed a truck with a hooped roof of new canvas, extra high.

"Look!" he said, pointing. Ida and Ping, who in the excitement of the elephants and the circus in general, had momentarily forgotten what they had come specially to see, gasped with a sudden rush of joy. "That must be HIS!" From this moment they were all agog. They moored the canoe and leaped out, urging Dr. Biggin to hurry. She looked at them quizzically, as if to say she didn't know they were such babies. But all she actually said, bringing out a tin from her pocket, was, "Have a bull's-eye. They calm the nerves."

They had good seats by the ring and sat there listening to the creaking ropes and the flapping of the ornamental scallops round the tiers of the roof, and the hubbub of people coming in, until the band began to play inside and drowned everything else.

When the show opened with an inrush of clowns, the children were positively sparking with excitement. One after another the clowns cartwheeled or somersaulted in, yelling, "Hola!" and tripping up on their trousers. But they were all midgets or little men, and before they had run out, the horses were there, plumed, reined-in, with round eyes and flaring nostrils, maneuvering without riders, scattering sawdust and foam as they tossed and pirouetted. Next, at a steamroller's pace, the elephants came on. They struck Ida as noble, wise, gentle, and merry—intelligent enough to do anything. But all that their trainers had been able to think of was to make them stand on their heads on low wooden stools. It was a sad thing to see. Afterward the biggest one was covered with a cloth painted like a bus. It stopped by a toy bus stop, and all the clowns clambered or sprang onto its back, clutching each other by the seat of the trousers or the ears or neckties till all were on somehow. The last, before leaping on, pulled the elephant's tail, on which was a bell, to set it in motion. It lumbered out holding a motor horn in its trunk and tooting as it went. These and other amusements, though they made the children laugh with everyone else, were not enough to quiet their fierce impatience for Terak. Ida, who had done theatricals at school, knew that he couldn't have had more than a few days to rehearse in. Perhaps he would only be a sideshow—sixpence to see the giant. And they had no more sixpences. It was a thought that spoiled several turns for her, including some Chinese acrobats who were sending Ping into a trance of approval as they flew through the air and landed as lightly as birds on each other's shoulders. The horses came in again, and then the lions. Turn after turn and still no Terak. There was the man who stands on a rolling ball, balances a chair by one leg on his forehead, and invites his lady friend in tights to climb up him and sit in it. It was all done so slowly and so carefully the children were mad with impatience.

At last the clowns ran in chattering like monkeys that are frightened and pointing backwards to the entrance passage. The children saw Terak first, leaping to their feet, waving and shouting, "There he is!" Their voices were drowned in the general clamor of surprise.

Terak was dressed in tartan trousers *and* a kilt, and a velvet jacket. His mother's bagpipes were under his arm. He was disguised with a red beard and hair and false eyebrows. His boots were four times as large as his feet and his sporran was as big as a bear cub. It was a shock to Ida that he did not look like himself. But there was no mistaking his eyes, or himself when he got going. It was an effort to take her attention off him even for a second, but she had to look to see how her Aunt Maud was taking it. Dr. Biggin was sitting at the very edge of the ring. With her round back, her arms crossed and hugging herself, and her nice wrinkled monkey face, she looked as if she might be one of the performers. She was watching with black shifting eyes, but not showing more interest than she had done in the other items. She was steadily sucking bull's-eyes.

Terak had the gift of stage presence, quite apart from his size. At his first appearance it was the size that had made everybody gasp. But oddly enough, though he had spent his life in unwilling invisibility, now that people saw him they could not look at anything else. He had a genius for making any silly little action both funny and lovable. The public took to him at sight and roared applause, which he acknowledged by blowing kisses and shaking himself by the hand, his incredible eyes creased up with joy at so much company. His own huge pleasure was in itself both ridiculous and infectious; it was a gathering snowball of success. The clowns, meanwhile, fooled around, shaking hands with each other, getting under his feet, and scattering with squawks when he shooed them, only to return. At last he cunningly caught them one by one, buzzing like flies, and after various attempts to get rid of them, he hung them up by their trousers or the back of their coats to hooks on the main tent poles. There they hung as if on a flypaper. His great wish, it seemed, was to make music, and for this purpose he had his bagpipes, which he continually dusted and caressed. But something was wrong. He could not get them to play. He blew and pumped, but either no sound came or the wrong one—a moaning foghorn, or a dreadful hee-haw just behind his ear, or a police whistle. At this last a clown with a blue helmet and a formidable rubber truncheon cycled in, looking for trouble but quite unable to see Terak, against whose legs he leaned his bicycle. Both he and it were lifted up and hung on a post, simply to leave the would-be musician in peace. After much tinkering and shaking, he drew out of the mouth-piece of his instrument the inevitable string of sausages and settled down to some soulful playing. Immediately, out of his pockets, his sleeves, the back of his coat collar, his sporran, came half a dozen wriggling dachshunds, howling their hearts out to the music. He pushed them all back again and again. He bribed them with sausages, but it was no good. In the end they all made music together in their own fashion, the clowns hanging up on the poles joining in with mouth organs, comb and paper, yodeling, whistles, or any percussion that their position allowed them to make. The audience could not resist joining in too, till Terak, rising to his full height, roared in a voice that would have silenced lions:

"SILENCE FOR THE ATOM BOMB!"

He held in his hand a shriveled balloon, which he began to inflate. Instantly there was dead silence. It was a giant-sized balloon, which slowly, slowly grew bigger. When it was beginning to get tight, Terak tried scratching it with his finger. At the squawk, out popped the dachshunds again, barking as if at a snake. They were silenced and treated one by one with puffs of air out of the balloon. Its diminished size was then inflated again to the same point and bigger. The tension and expectation were kept up so long that the audience became quite hysterical. The clowns hanging on the poles kicked and pleaded for mercy as the balloon grew fabulously, filling the space of the ring and bouncing and wobbling on its mouthpiece. Terak seemed frightened of it himself. He brought it to his mouth for another blow, then let a little out instead. He became madly brave, taking in a last huge lungful and addressing himself to the balloon with distended cheeks. It exploded with a bang so loud, you could hardly hear it. Terak went over on his back. The hooked-up clowns whizzed down to earth (they were all on pulleys) and ran for their lives, leaving their coats and trousers on the hooks. The dachshunds swarmed out to lick Terak's face, and by an unrehearsed accident two of them ran off to have a tug-of-war over his beard, which had come off. And there was Terak sitting up with his own face exposed, blowing kisses to Ping, Oskar, and Ida and tossing them spare balloons. Before they could do anything but grin back, the midget clowns rushed in again with a strawberry net, which they threw over Terak's head and tied with ropes. Then an elephant was brought in to drag him away.

This was the end of the program. The audience stood up to clap. They stamped and shouted, "Terak! We want Terak!"

The children turned to each other. "Isn't he having a wonderful time! Let's go and talk to him." Then they remembered that this was a benefit appearance for Dr. Biggin.

"What do you think of the giant?" they asked, but at that moment "God Save the Queen" began, and everybody had to stand up and be quiet. When it was over, they all began again. "What did you think of the giant? Were you surprised? That proves it, doesn't it? No one can say your tooth isn't real now."

Dr. Biggin smiled knowingly and condescendingly. "I enjoyed him immensely. He was a really wonderful fake."

"Fake!" cried the children, appalled. "He was real, as real as anything. Didn't you see his face when the dogs pulled his beard off? Didn't you see his teeth, like your tooth?"

"The rest of him was just as false as his beard. They can fake anything nowadays. There aren't teeth like the one I found. That was the whole point of it. Probably this was a man on stilts, padded. It's an old trick."

"But Aunt Maud! His eyes! They are as big as horses' eyes and all laughing. And he saw us."

"Probably done with magnifying lenses. But it doesn't matter how it was done. We weren't meant to spot it."

"Let's go and find him, and then you will see."

"My dear children! I almost envy you your credulity! We won't go and find him, firstly, because they would never allow us to see how it was done, and secondly, because if they did, it would be the first big disillusionment of your young lives. A heap of gadgets and an empty suit."

"But we thought you believed in giants."

"I believe there were giants once—twenty thousand years ago. But not now. There aren't any now. Because if there were, we should know, shouldn't we? They're not things you could overlook."

"But . . ." said the children, but gave it up in despair.

As they were walking back to the canoes, each with a large ice cream Dr. Biggin had fallen behind to pay for, Ida said, "I'm sorry, Ping. One can't do anything for grown-ups. They're hopeless."

Ping sighed. "I can't understand—when it's the thing they want most in the world and it's there before their eyes—why they won't see it."

"They are often like that," said Oskar wisely. "They don't like *now*. If it's really interesting, it has to be *then*."

Other books in the Odyssey series:

L. M. Boston
- [ ] THE CHILDREN OF GREEN KNOWE
- [ ] TREASURE OF GREEN KNOWE
- [ ] THE RIVER AT GREEN KNOWE
- [ ] AN ENEMY AT GREEN KNOWE
- [ ] A STRANGER AT GREEN KNOWE

Edward Eager
- [ ] HALF MAGIC
- [ ] KNIGHT'S CASTLE
- [ ] MAGIC BY THE LAKE
- [ ] MAGIC OR NOT?
- [ ] SEVEN-DAY MAGIC

Mary Norton
- [ ] THE BORROWERS

John R. Tunis
- [ ] THE KID FROM TOMKINSVILLE
- [ ] WORLD SERIES
- [ ] ALL-AMERICAN
- [ ] YEA! WILDCATS!
- [ ] A CITY FOR LINCOLN

Virginia Hamilton
- [ ] A WHITE ROMANCE
- [ ] JUSTICE AND HER BROTHERS
- [ ] DUSTLAND
- [ ] THE GATHERING

Look for these titles and others in the Odyssey series in your local bookstore.

Or send prepayment in the form of a check or money order to: HBJ (Operator J) 465 S. Lincoln Drive, Troy, Missouri 63379.

Or call: 1-800-543-1918 (ask for Operator J).

I've enclosed my check payable to Harcourt Brace Jovanovich.

Charge my: [ ] Visa [ ] MasterCard
           [ ] American Express

Card Expiration Date _____

| | | | | | | | | | | | | | | | | |
Card #

Signature _____

Phone _____

Address _____

_____ State ___ Zip ___

Please send me _____ copy/copies @ $3.95 each

($3.95 x no. of copies) $_____

Subtotal $_____

Your state sales tax   + $_____

Shipping and handling   + $_____
($1.50 x no. of copies)

Total $_____

PRICES SUBJECT TO CHANGE